Love at First Wild

Love at First Wild

A GRUMPY CURVY GIRL / EX-MILITARY MOUNTAIN MAN ROMANCE

ROUGH & READY COUNTRY
BOOK TWELVE

ENGRID EAVES

Join the Engrid Eaves Community!

RUGGED, POSSESSIVE COWBOY MOUNTAIN MEN.
HEADSTRONG, COURAGEOUS, CURVY GIRLS.
STEAMY, SATISFYING HAPPILY EVER AFTERS.
GIVEAWAYS. FREEBIES.
NEW RELEASES. LATEST NEWS.

Subscribe to my newsletter today to never miss out on a new
steamy, small-town read.
SIGN UP FOR MY NEWSLETTER

Trigger Warning

This book contains content/themes that may not be suitable for all readers, including kidnapping, violence, and discussion and depictions of human trafficking with brief mention of the abuses associated with it.

Please read at your own discretion.

Chapter One

PAIGE

I stare at the text message, my eyes narrowing and my head swirling.

> It's about time somebody taught you a lesson

The threatening rant doesn't end there...

> Hope you're all paid up on your life insurance

> Of course, good luck with that. They'll never find your body, fucking whore

I shake my head, worry gripping my stomach. After years of producing true crime-inspired, unscripted documentaries, more popularly known as reality TV, a weird cult of elders in black and white suits with piety advertised on their faces are what will finally get me?

The thought is laughable against the backdrop of serial killers, spousal murderers, and con people I've dealt with in the past. But then again, I never stumbled across a scandal as big as what has started to emerge among the ruling elite of the House of the Seven Prophets.

That said, I can't say with certainty who the texts come from as the number is unlisted. But I know where to wager my money. And the texts didn't start until I dug deep into the large cult-like organization that stretches across the West Coast, discovering scandals like polygamy, pedophilia, and child marriage.

I stand, handing my phone across a large wooden desk for Phil Conners, executive director of In the Haystack production company.

Phil is tall and thin with salt-and-pepper hair and a large, hooked nose. His eyes are grayish blue, and they round as he reads, shaking his head. "We have to turn this over to the appropriate authorities."

I nod in full agreement, already fatalistic about the outcome. I shrug, saying resignedly, "Nothing I've shown local police so far has gone anywhere. I honestly feel like they're stonewalling."

He takes a deep breath, making his cheeks puff out on the exhale. "What a wicked web this supposed religion of peace weaves."

As I reach back over the desk to retrieve my phone, Phil crosses his arms, deep in thought. The corners of his mouth turn down as he levels his gaze on me, his face more haggard and wrinkled than usual. "Be sure to keep a journal detailing everything and continue forwarding things to law enforcement and the company attorneys. I don't want this to blow up in the company's face or harm you in any way."

Phil has acted like a mentor to me ever since I started working for In the Haystack after graduating from film school nine years ago. And Meredith, his wife, is as close to a caring, loving mom as I'll probably ever get. "The offer stands if you'd like to come stay at our place until this blows over. You can't beat our security, and Meredith will obviously go to whatever lengths it takes to make you feel welcome in the guest house."

"Thank you," I say, trying to infuse my voice with the gratitude his offer inspires. "But I can't let Mortimer Cady and the House of the Seven Prophets intimidate me. If I cave this easily, after a handful of empty threats, I won't have a very long career in gritty reality TV, will I?"

"Your career should never come at the expense of your safety, Paige," he reminds somberly. "Besides, how can you be so certain these threats are empty?"

"It's the group's MO. They rule through fear and intimidation. But most of their threats have no teeth. At least, according to the witnesses I've interviewed over the past few years."

"That's a dangerous gamble. Besides, Meredith would love the company. Ever since the nest has emptied, she's been lonely and looking for companionship. I guess an old fart like me isn't enough."

I laugh at the marathon-running, extremely fit man. "If you're an old fart, then the rest of the world is more or less grave-bound." Although I'm joking, the word *grave* incites a strange, nauseous feeling. "Thank you very much for your offer. But I can't let this guy or his gang of religious zealots shake me."

"I knew you were going to say that," he replies, a cat's-got-his-tongue expression seizing his face. "So, I have a plan B, and this one is non-negotiable."

My stomach roils. "What?"

"I don't know how well the office grapevine is working these days, but Steph managed to break her ankle earlier today, and it requires surgery."

3

"Ouch," I wince. "How did she do that?"

"She was wearing high heels of some sort and misjudged the distance to the sidewalk's curb, rolling her ankle."

My eyebrows hit my hairline.

"As in, there was a lot of bleeding, and she's going in for emergency surgery in the morning. Something about putting in screws and plates to stabilize everything."

"That sounds nightmarish."

"You're telling me."

"Anyway, she's recently been working on a project for a reality TV show featuring this YouTuber called the Military Mountain Man. You ever heard of him?"

I shake my head, amused he would even ask me such a question.

He nods. "I know that's not generally your thing. But every now and again, you go all granola-munching backpacker on me, so I thought I'd ask." By *granola-munching backpacker*, I assume he's referring to the mini camping vacays I take to Yosemite, Mount Whitney, and other cool wilderness destinations any chance I get. I love being outdoors more than anything.

That said, I'm no survivalist prepper. But I nod anyway, not wanting to split hairs with my very good-natured, though sometimes stern, boss.

"It's not true crime-related, though," I stammer.

"Don't you think you could use a little break from true crime? Besides, this assignment will help you get your mind on other things and explore the possibilities. After all, there's far more to reality TV than criminal minds."

"True. But jumping to outdoorsman survival hardly seems like a close fit." Although I owe my career to Phil, I fight his decision with special vehemence because I know what comes next. Assignment of cameramen. There's only one choice for this kind of shoot: Johnny Rodriguez. I went to film school

4

with the guy, and he's a consummate professional when it comes to wildlife and nature documentaries, but he's also creepy and overbearing. Coupled with the fact we briefly dated years ago, I want to avoid him at all costs.

"There's no better closer than you, Paige. Military Mountain Man, a.k.a. Ridge Dawson, has proven himself quite difficult regarding negotiations. We need somebody to pin him down, something I'm not certain Steph would've been able to pull off, broken ankle or not. You, on the other hand, will get his signature. I don't have a doubt in my mind."

The corners of my mouth turn up though I remain unconvinced. "I don't know, Phil. You may have found the limit of my negotiation skills."

"There's only one way to find out, and it isn't by debating in my office."

"True."

"And this will get you away from SoCal and any nefarious plans Cady may have in the works. Hopefully, it'll give law enforcement some time to rethink their handling of this case, too."

It amuses me to hear how Phil tries to spin this to make it sound beneficial to me. But then, why should it surprise me? I learned all my best negotiation strategies from him. And he and Meredith have been so kind and generous to me over the years that even though I want with every ounce of my being to decline, I can't.

"Johnny will accompany you—"

My glare stops Phil mid-speech. "If the man hasn't signed a contract yet, why does Johnny have to tag along?"

"It was a very specific part of Military Mountain Man's negotiations. He wants to meet the person who'll be working most closely with."

I nod. "Makes sense." I hate admitting this, though.

"We already have him working on accommodations in

5

Hollister, which is the closest town with amenities to Rough & Ready Country."

"Rough & Ready Country? Seriously?"

He nods, running his hand pensively over his chin. "Indeed. Don't fall in love with a cowboy or mountain man while you're there."

"No chance." I laugh. "Rednecks and hicks have never been my thing." I don't know if any man's my thing, to be honest. I seem incapable of making a relationship work, largely because I always have to wear the figurative pants in it. Finding a capable man I can respect to protect me, care for me, *and* commit? Impossible. The best way to describe my experiences with the dating scene are lonely and disenchanting.

"No, I can't imagine they have." He laughs at the ridiculousness of the suggestion. "I'll have Judy email you some links to Military Mountain Man's YouTube channel and Steph's sizzle reel. I would appreciate it if you could watch those before leaving."

I exhale, looking at my watch. "What time do we need to head out tomorrow?"

"Well, it's a seven-hour drive, but nine hours if you hit rush hour."

"Tomorrow's Saturday, Phil."

"Is it?" he asks, running his hand through his hair. "This week has me frazzled."

"You're telling me."

"Anyway, you'll need to leave first thing in the morning. I'll let you coordinate the details with Johnny. This YouTuber's been tough to nail down for a meeting and even more difficult to negotiate with, so Sunday's appointment is of paramount importance."

"I'll do what I can, but I have the Keep the Earth Green charity event tonight. So, I won't be able to watch any of Military Mountain Man's videos until Saturday night after we arrive."

"Yes, I forgot about that. Either way, as long as you get a sense of his style of videos before the meeting that should be fine. Otherwise, I'll leave you to it as our top closer."

"Really?" I say, arching an eyebrow. "I know I'm good, but the top?

"Really."

"Then, where's my bonus?" I ask teasingly.

"You get Ridge Dawson on the hook, and it'll be well worth your while. I promise."

I shake my head. "You and Meredith have already done so much for me—"

"No, seriously. This guy's going to be our next Bear Grylls or *Survivorman*. And between you and me, I think the show will need more finessing than Steph's currently capable of. So, if you come back with a signed contract, consider the show officially yours."

My jaw drops. "B-b-but Steph would kill me."

"Nope, I have it on good word there's another show she's far more interested in producing. Think single, performing arts, stage dads looking for love."

My head spins at the bizarre juxtaposition. "Like *Dance Moms* meets *The Bachelor?*"

"Exactly."

"Why not throw in the whole kit and caboodle and make the dads get married without meeting their fiancées beforehand?" I joke, but the sad part of me notes I may be among the first show participants. After all, my prospects are non-existent at this point.

Phil's face lights up to my shock. "That's a fantastic idea!"

"I'm being sarcastic," I say under my breath, staring at my boss.

"I know," he replies in the same voice. "Now get out of here and go kick ass in that meeting."

I stride from his office until a thought hits me. Tipping my head and upper body back in and holding onto the door-frame, I correct, "And just so we're on the same page, I haven't agreed to any of this yet. I'm not done with the House of the Seven Prophets. Please consider letting me finish what I started."

"It's not worth risking your life. Keep me apprised of the situation, and let me know if you receive any more harassing texts. That said, I'm hoping this will all blow over with you temporarily out of the spotlight."

"Me, too." I frown, suddenly feeling very small, vulnerable, and alone in the world. I wish I had parents who actually cared about me and wanted to know what is going on in my life. I wish I had a boyfriend or husband who loved and protected me. There's a lot I wish for that I've put on the back burner for my career, which makes the thought of backing down to the House of the Seven Prophets infuriating and impossible.

But Phil and Meredith are about as close as I'll ever get to family, and I can't speak to her in confidence about the situation without it inevitably getting back to my boss. I can't blame her for this. I know she wants to keep me safe. But I want to do the same for the young women and children in this cult who don't have anyone speaking or advocating for them.

Seven and a half hours in from Los Angeles to Hollister, I'm so over the driving. It doesn't help that I've used this time to pore back over various interviews I did with eyewitnesses to events associated with the House of the Seven Prophets.

I've listened to these interviews numerous times and examined the transcripts. But I continue to look for tiny details in case I've missed the one thing that could break the case wide open. At the heart of everything is Mortimer Cady, a part of the church's hierarchy of elders. An appropriate title for him would be the enforcer. One interviewee after another relates vicious stories about the man I first encountered while working on my unscripted documentary of the organization.

Like me, they were initially put at ease by Cady's unimpressive height—all of five foot seven, chubby physique, and unmemorable face. But when things went south, and he came collecting, the mannerly facade and non-threatening persona quickly gave way to a venom-spitting monster who relied on verbal abuse smattered with words like "whore" and "bitch" to demoralize and wear down his victims.

Some victims also mention his use of burner phones and third-party harassment to put people in line. They recall him mentioning that he hoped they had their life insurance paid up. I rub my temples, thinking back on the recent threatening texts. They have Cady's stamp all over them.

A couple of the interviews put a thick knot of dread in my throat, especially with people who left the cult and had to deal with the consequences. Intimidation and threats mark the first line of offense. But tactics ratchet up over time. One survivor describes being run off the road by a member in good standing with the church. Another discusses vicious texts and emails she received with clear warnings not to speak to me. A handful have faced gunpoint threats, and then there are those who disappeared or died under mysterious circumstances...

Each of the whistleblowers who spoke to me face the same threats and reprimands. So, how can I let them down at the first sign of trouble? After hours of listening to testimony, my brain feels numb, and I need a break. Thankfully, Hollister is only twenty miles away. Never have I felt so elated to finally reach a podunk little dot on the Northern California map.

The interview I'm listening to goes silent for a moment, letting me know I'm receiving a text. I glance quickly at my phone, seeing it's from Johnny. He left a bit before me this morning, so I assume he's already at the bed and breakfast where we'll be staying for the next couple of nights.

I pull over at the first embankment that I see, endless winding two-lane roads marking the final leg of my journey. Opening my text app, I click on Johnny's last message, replying and launching a conversation in real-time.

> We have a problem...

Yes?

> There's only one room available

One room? What are you talking about?

> Exactly what I said

Shit

I shake my head, not in the kind of mood to deal with his manipulations. The dude's never gotten over his college crush on me or our brief crash-and-burn attempt at dating that lasted all of a few weeks. For me, it was nothing to write home about. For him? Well, I don't know what it was for him.

But he keeps trying to find a way back into my pants while simultaneously getting angry and creepy when I rebuff his unwanted advances. Passive aggression and delusion at its finest. That's why I avoid him like the plague. Texting Steph, I ask:

How's the ankle?

> It's seen better days

> Surgery went well?

> > Yep, and I'm high as a kite on pain pills, so disregard anything weird that I might say

An X-ray comes over the phone, showing an ankle joint with two plates and at least thirteen screws.

> Yikes! Is this the new Million Dollar Man version of you?

> > Fancy, isn't it?

> Insanity. How did you do that again?

> > More or less walking

Steph has always been a little clumsy. I hate to admit it, and she's prone to breaking bones. But this is the first time one of her injuries has led to surgery.

> You need to take care of yourself

> > Will do. Lover boy's making sure I keep my ankle iced and my blood streaming with pain pills

> Good man

> > The best

> You owe me, btw

> > How so?

> For making me work with Johnny

> > Oh, shit. How's that going so far?

As bad as usual. Somehow the bed and breakfast we're staying at only has one room booked for the both of us. One bed, too, I'd imagine

Are you freaking serious?

Yep

Make sure Phil knows about this

Oh, I will

A horn blares behind me, making me jump in the seat of my inky black Fiat 124 Spider. Looking in the rearview mirror, I see a large white dually with an angry-looking driver staring at me. The truck is big enough to drive over my diminutive vehicle, monster-truck style.

Have to go. Talk later

My whole body shakes as I throw the phone on the passenger seat, shifting into drive. Am I parked in the wrong spot? My heart races. My mind follows.

Bile rises in my throat as my stomach roils, and I watch the truck jump back onto the roadway behind me, following so closely I'm certain he's about to rear-end me. He continues to blare his horn, flipping me off and screaming. I can't hear the words, but his face rages, red as a beet.

Oh my God! What do I do? The interviews I listened to on the way here wash over me. Especially the story of the woman who was driven off the road. The truck's engine roars behind me, his horn screeching as I naturally put my foot on the gas, trying in vain to put some distance between us. But the man is relentless. Each time I pull forward enough to read his license plate, he follows suit, surging to close the gap between us.

Do I call the police? My eyes flicker to the mirror again, observing his features so that I can easily give a description to the cops. Long, strawberry blond beard, beady eyes, thin face, even thinner lips and a bulbous, puggish nose.

Suddenly, the truck accelerates, and I reflexively swerve onto the embankment, thankfully finding a swatch of bare dirt and slamming on my brakes just in time to avoid a large Ponderosa pine. The truck roars past, the driver still laying on the horn as he speeds away, and I clutch my chest. This trip is already a nightmare, and I haven't even made it to the Hollister city limits yet.

Chapter Two

RIDGE

"Well, if it isn't the celebrity!" Logan exclaims with a frown as I stand next to his table at Stonie's, finally gaining his attention. The big, black-haired, bearded mountain man stands unceremoniously, his brown eyes snapping as he envelopes me in a bear hug.

My other brothers rise to greet me, too. All six feet five inches of Wolfe, the only one who equals me in height, and Hawk, the pretty boy with his thick mane of raven's black hair, tanned skin, and high cheekbones that the girls can't get enough of. Both hug me heartily, bidding me to take the empty seat at their table.

"How are my three boring-as-hell brothers? Family life treating you well?

"Living the dream," Wolfe says with a big grin. The clean-shaven Army Ranger turned cowboy means it from his annoy-ing, infectious smile to the spark of delight never far from his brooding eyes. I can't blame him. He and his wife, Izzie, nearly divorced a couple of years ago. Things got messy as hell in family court as they fought for custody of my niece and nephew, trying not to admit what everyone in the family already knew. They were still madly in love with each other and needed to work things out. Fortunately, they did, which is part of why I'm amazed to see him here today.

"How'd you get away from diaper duty?" He and Izzie welcomed their third baby, Maverick, a few weeks ago. In fact, this is the first time my Army Ranger brother has been out since the birth.

"Izzie's sister and niece came into town to lend a hand, so I thought I'd break away while I could. Besides, it's not every day you've got a fucking reality television star in your midst."

I shrug, frowning and shaking my head. "Well, we'll see how the meeting goes."

"Next thing you know," Hawk says with a quiet laugh. "You'll have girls throwing their panties at you when you walk through the grocery store." The reserved Sho-Ban helicopter pilot has never had a problem with the ladies, although he's now a very happily married man, thanks to reuniting with his sweetheart, our good childhood friend, Roxy.

"Is that what it's like for you, Hawk?"

He crosses his arms, sitting back in his chair and taking everything I say far too seriously. Like he always does. It's not that Hawk doesn't have a sense of humor, but he's generally straightforward and direct, so he expects the same from the world. The corners of his mouth turn down. "Nope, never had that experience, and Roxy would beat the hell out of me if I ever did." A lopsided grin captures his face at the end, and I can't begrudge my brother his happiness. Lord knows he waited long enough to claim Roxy.

We all laugh, filling the empty bar with deep-throated chuckles.

"So, when's the official meeting with that TV producer?" Wolfe asks mischievously. He knows this question will get my hackles up.

"Tomorrow morning."

"TV producer?" Logan asks, looking glassy-eyed. "What am I missing?"

Wolfe and Hawk stare at him quizzically for a moment before the burly Army Ranger exclaims jovially. "Oh, that's right! You've been so busy changing diapers and dealing with spitup that you haven't heard the latest with Ridge." Logan and Jess recently had a baby, too.

"There is no latest," I grumble, not ready to explain this again.

But Logan's dark eyes bore into mine. "Do tell," he says with that older brother command that annoys the hell out of me.

"It's nothing," I shrug, but I can tell by his face my answer isn't about to satisfy him. "Fuck," I groan, shaking my head. All eyes are on me now, which is the last thing I like dealing with. There's a reason I've hopped from one solitary profession to the next. Despite my YouTube channel, I'm generally a man of few words who hates being put on the spot. "Couldn't we focus on the last elk hunt I led or something more interesting?"

"Spill your guts," Logan commands, and I furrow my brows.

"So, there's this—" Wolfe starts for me. Fuck, if I'm going to let him make this any stupider than it already is.

Butting in, I say, "I've been getting calls from this production studio who wants to sign me for a reality TV show based on my channel and the outfitting I do for clients. It's really not that big a deal. And nothing's for sure. The agreements they've presented so far don't really suit me, but they're sending representatives out tomorrow morning. Supposedly to sweeten the contract terms."

Wolfe ribs me. "Before we know it, you'll be the most famous among us."

"Not with Zane and Rock around." Zane's a professional

16

bull rider who once topped the circuits, earning lots of fame and buckle bunnies, and Rock's a well-known tattoo artist and singer/musician.

Logan stares off into space, looking exhausted. So, I put a hand on his shoulder, asking, "Are you okay, dude?"

He scrubs his hand over his face. "Yeah, I'm okay. Just had a long night of searching for those two missing hikers who had their faces plastered all over town."

"Yeah, I heard you found them this morning. Congrats."

He pauses for a moment, looking like he's about to doze off, before answering gruffly, "Max is the one who found them, not me. I'm just the guy who gives the commands and treats." Logan is a search and rescue lead who trains canines for avalanche recovery during the winter and various types of retrievals during the summer. In fact, he rescued his lovely blonde-haired wife, Jess, on one of his missions, sealing the deal with her.

Logan says, "The offer still stands if you're ready to leave behind social media and snooty-ass hunters. Your wilderness survival and tracking skills would be priceless." He works as the lead at Sierra Search and Rescue, and he's long beat his drum about hiring me. But I need to do my own thing. It's always been that way. It's one of the main drivers behind how I ended up a Scout Sniper in the Corps.

"Nah, bro. The outfitter business is as lucrative as ever. And now that I'm bringing in new audiences with the survivalist videos. I'm not tempted to switch careers."

"Your loss," he says, crossing his arms.

"And your gain," Hawk chimes in. "Ridge is the orneriest, most feral mountain man in the Sierra Nevada backcountry. He'd probably scare anybody he tried to rescue half to death, convincing them they're a Bigfoot abduction victim."

Wolfe laughs, and I frown. "Funny."

I notice in my peripheral vision Logan's eyes have closed,

17

and his head is leaning forward. Otherwise, the motherfucker would gladly be in the midst of the gentle ribbing going on with my foster brothers.

I cock my head to the side. "I'm no Bigfoot. And I'm also no nine-to-fiver. Hell, I'd rather go back to sniping."

"Back to sniping?" Logan grumbles, lifting his head and scrubbing his eyes with his palms some more. "Is that even a career option?"

"No," Wolfe says firmly, shaking his head with a grimace. "Although if you need to feel the action again, you're always more than welcome to a job at my security company."

"Security company? How long are you planning on keeping that ruse up?" I ask, laughing as our waitress, Florence, approaches the table again, devouring me with her eyes. I ignore her less-than-subtle body language. Never been the kind of man who settles for casual hookups, which makes my perpetual singlehood akin to celibacy. But I'm picky when it comes to women. Always have been, and I swore after the last bad breakup that I won't settle for anything less than the one.

Unfortunately, with so many of my foster brothers now happily married and in the family way, it makes me feel lone-lier than ever. Smiling genuinely at the busty brunette with bedroom eyes that contain every red flag known to man, I ask politely, "Ma'am, I'll take another Rough & Ready Red." It's the local ale, made by my brother Axel in small batches. Nothing satisfies quite the same.

She puts her hand on her hip. "Ma'am? Now, how'd you forget my name is 'darlin'?" She winks, popping her bubblegum in her mouth. Trouble, trouble, trouble. From head to toe, but I'd be lying if I said the female attention didn't put a warm spot in my core. "Is that all you want, big boy?" she asks, leaning down to whisper the last two words in my ear. We all went to the same middle and high school although she's a handful of years younger than me. But hell, if she doesn't keep getting flirtier as each of my foster brothers settles down.

There are fifteen of us total, although Holden's doing time in the clink. But even he's got a girl ... kind of. She's a saucy redhead named Delilah who owns the only café in town, The Human Being. That said, I don't know if they're still technically a couple.

It's been years of separation now, and she's far too pretty to stay single forever. Or wait for a scumbag, which my brother unfortunately was before entering prison. I imagine he still is, seeing how well reformation behind bars tends to go.

As for the one-hundred percent single ones, all that's left are Axel, Bowie, and me. No wonder they never come into town, let alone to Stonie's. Florence makes me feel a bit like a rainforest tourist dropped headfirst into a piranha-infested river.

"Yes. Another beer's all I want," I say in my politest voice with a firm nod of the head. The waitress eyes my brothers, observing their nearly full bottles.

"What a shame," she replies, biting her bottom lip and staring at me in a way that makes me feel so uncomfortable I run my finger along the collar of my flannel shirt to let off a bit of the steam. Not good steam but hot nonetheless. "I love those survival videos you make, by the way. The one about surviving in your car during a blizzard is so good."

I nod. "I made that for Alex, Maksim's wife." Maksim's our youngest brother, and he met his wife, Alex, after saving her from her SUV in the middle of a freak March blizzard. The poor woman nearly froze to death because she didn't have the knowledge she needed. It was part of the impetus for my YouTube channel.

"Hope for the best, and prepare for the worst," I reply.

She giggles, an odd response to that phrase. "If I find a

Sharpie, will you sign the girls later?" She cups her tits with her hands, pressing them together and making each of my brothers dutifully avert their eyes. I remember a time when Logan and Hawk would've been all over this. As for Wolfe, he's been with Izzie for so long that I can't remember him ever having eyes on anyone else.

My brows shoot up into my hairline as I reply quickly, careful to look at her face, "Ma'am, you must have mistaken me for my brother, Rock. I'm no rockstar."

Logan shoots me a warning look, shaking his head.

Fuck. I almost forgot. That tattooed hellion's taken now, too, and apparently living it up with a sweet little rockabilly kitten. I stare at my hands, refusing to take in the expression on Florence's face or continue our conversation until she takes a hint and leaves.

I sigh with relief. After all, I'm a thirsty man, not a hungry one. And by thirst, I mean one of Axel's delicious beverages. "I can't believe Rock's a committed man now, too. Fuck, you guys are ruining me here. I never thought I'd end up the monk in the family."

"You kind of have to come out of the woods every now and again to meet living, breathing human women, Ridge. It's not like they hang out in the middle of nowhere," Logan counters grumpily, running his hand through his black hair.

"I'm here with you guys right now."

"Yeah, for the first time in forever. The last time we saw your ass was at the ranch's Christmas Eve party, and you didn't even stay long enough to hear Rock and Effie sing together." Apparently, Rock's new woman is a fellow guitarist and singer, and everyone swears their duets are epic.

"A bad storm was blowing in. You know how inaccessible my cabin is in the best of weather. But that blizzard was no fun driving in," I excuse. "Besides, what woman was I going to meet at that party? You guys have taken all the good ones." My voice sounds more exasperated than I want it to as I spit out the last statement.

"I think Logan was more making a point about your lack of social activities in general," Hawk adds drily.

"I know," Wolfe adds with a laugh. "Maybe you should try what Rock said Fierce did."

I shake my head, my mind spinning. I always tend to forget that Rock is friends with one of the shit-kicking asshole Amestoys. I hate those fucking Basque sheepherders, always grazing their sheep on our land and causing trouble for my family. "Why in the hell does Rock still talk to that dumbass?"

Wolfe shrugs. "Well, he is Fierce's tattoo artist."

"I guess that ink slinger will do anything for money," I grumble.

"No, from what Rock tells me, they're actually friends, though I don't get it."

"What else would I expect from Rock?" I say, shaking my head. He always gave Dad more trouble than he was worth, even though I love my inked foster brother as much as the rest. "So, what the fuck did Fierce do?" I ask, stroking my beard and slightly annoyed I'm curious enough to even ask.

"He ordered a woman off the internet."

"He ordered a woman?" I scrunch my face.

Wolfe nods.

But Logan shakes his head. "Jess knows Felicity, and it wasn't like that. They met on a dating site called Mountain Mates."

"I take it Felicity's the girl?" I've never met Felicity, and I already feel sorry for her. But truth be told, I feel even sorrier for myself.

Hawk adds quietly, "I heard Axel's on Mountain Mates, too. Talking to some girl named Aspen, and it's getting kind of serious. Guess his brewing business is lonely without a partner."

"Axel, too?" I shake my head, studying the bottle rings on the dingy wooden table where we sit. "Well, I guess if Rock and Fierce can find women, it's good enough for Axel, too. But shit, if I'm the last bachelor standing..." I pause, trying to wrap my head around it all. "What the fuck's wrong with me?" I lament at the worst possible moment as Florence returns, impatiently handing me my drink.

"That's a very good question," she comments spunkily, swaying her hips. "What in the hell is wrong with you?"

Hawk leans forward, smiling politely. "I'll take another Corona, please." The move instantly takes Florence's eyes off me as she greedily eyes Hawk. Women have always gone gaga for him. So, he ignores it with ease, unlike me, who tends to get a little flustered. "Thank you," he concludes, finishing the conversation before it starts with his guarded tone of voice.

She shakes her head, side-glancing at Logan before whispering audibly under her breath. "This town used to be so much more fun."

"Thank you for the rescue," I say, nodding toward the helicopter pilot.

"I always was good at providing air cover for you jarheads."

"Can't argue with that, brother," I say as I raise my icy-cold beer bottle, and my brothers follow.

The door to Stonie's opens, and a man and woman walk in. The shock of the glare from the late afternoon sun makes me squint as I turn, observing the duo.

My heart immediately drops into my stomach with a kathunk. I'm pretty damn sure the thinly populated bar just heard the hollow noise. I stare at a raven-haired angel, thick and dressed to the nines. The lines of her black, below-the-knee, tight-fitting skirt and matching jacket with a silky white blouse have a buttoned-up vibe. Everything about her outfit is immaculate, professional, and so well tailored that it tempts my imagination to sexy speculation.

A long current of glossy, raven-hued hair flows down her back, and her pouty, generous lips are cherry-stained. Her large, expressive mahogany-colored eyes catch mine, knocking the wind from my chest. I sputter on the sip of beer I just took, coughing and wheezing like a goddamned fool.

"No wonder you're still single," Hawk teases under his breath, and Wolfe and Logan nod in silent agreement.

Chapter Three

PAIGE

I should've known better. I *did* know better. Mentally, I kick myself as Johnny, the cameraman on this ill-fated mission, and I walk from Hollister's one bed and breakfast to the only bar in town, Stonie's. I rub my temples as we walk, so grumpy I can't string two words together or remove the frown that's captured my lips.

My insides still shake, and my heart races every time I think about the truck driver who pushed me off the roadway. I've already filed a report with the sheriff's department, but I never got a full license plate, and my description of the driver remains fairly generic. Everything happened so fast, but I can't shake the growing suspicion Cady is somehow behind this.

At moments like this, I feel completely vulnerable to the world. What I wouldn't give to have a man who could hold and comfort me, like Steph's boyfriend, Tom, who she affectionately refers to as "lover boy." Instead, I'm stuck with a creep who raises the hairs on the back of my neck, waiting for the next shoe to fall in whatever game the House of the Seven Prophets is playing with me.

I don't begrudge Steph, but this trip has already been a

shit show on so many levels, culminating in the botched-up bed and breakfast booking. Not only is there one room and one bed, but it's the honeymoon suite. For God's sake! How do you accidentally book the honeymoon suite?

"Come on, Paige. We're both adults, and it's just for a couple of nights." His voice is a nasal whine that makes my skin crawl.

His words make me stop in the middle of Main Street. In SoCal, this move would be a death wish. But in sleepy Hollister, I have a feeling Johnny and I are the most exciting thing that's happened all day. And more or less the only traffic.

"Out of the question!"

"So, what? Are you going to sleep in your car?"

I glare at him. "No, but you are."

He lets out a loud groan, and I continue walking. "Seriously?"

"Seriously!" My high-heeled shoes hammer across the pavement, reaching the cement sidewalk where I suddenly flip back around towards him. "If you had anything to do with this—"

"Whoa! Are you accusing me of sabotaging this trip?"

I arch an eyebrow. "I am accusing you of fucking up our room booking."

"And where's your proof?" he hisses, his eyes narrowing.

I throw my hands up in the air. "Well, then, explain to me what happened."

Silence.

"This just sucks all around!"

"Paige, it'll be fine. It's really not that big a deal."

"Not a big deal?" I question, putting my hands on my hips. "We are coworkers. It is absolutely a big deal."

"Maybe you should drive to Ophir City, then. They must have cheap motels there."

The thought of driving again today makes me feel

nauseous. "Johnny, you're not listening. We are not sharing a room, and since you were responsible for booking our rooms, you will be the one to find alternate accommodations if Mrs. Chatterton can't work something out."

The little old lady who owns the B&B is as sweet as lemon meringue pie and said she'd do what she can to find other accommodations for us. Something tells me this would involve staying in a private home, which I refuse to do ... *ever*. After all, I've produced too many true crime reality docuseries to take anyone's kindness at face value.

"You are so fucking unreasonable," Johnny exclaims.

"Watch it. Need I remind you I'm technically your supervisor?" I level my gaze on him.

"You had to pull that one, didn't you? Why are you suddenly on this assignment anyway? I thought you stuck to serial rapists and killers."

"I told you," I answer grumpily, trying to keep my cool. I hate it when people push my buttons because it makes me feel and act out of control. "I replaced Steph." He knows the rest, so I save my breath.

Everything about this assignment has already taken me well outside of my comfort zone. I know next to nothing about the guy we're approaching. I haven't watched any of his videos, although I plan on binge-watching them tonight.

Even without the prep, however, I'm confident in my abilities. I turn my persuasive skills on Johnny to ensure the hotel booking is mine. "Johnny, you're an avid outdoors cameraman. You've camped in the Sahara, for crying out loud. You can spend a couple of nights in your van."

"Steph has yet to pin this guy down to anything. What's so special about you?"

"I have my ways," I grumble.

Entering the poorly lit place with dollar bills stuck to every inch of the ceiling. I don't have especially high hopes for the food or the company. But what do I expect in a redneck town of two thousand? The only place more inadequately equipped for visitors would be my hometown.

I scan the dingy bar, seeing a huge hulk of a man with a long dark beard behind the bar who, intuition tells me, is the eponymous Stonie. Most of the tables are empty, though the big-screen TV broadcasts images of motorcycle racing in a large stadium. A jukebox in the back corner glows invitingly, filling me with nostalgia. I haven't seen one of those in a while, and the billiards table next to it is threadbare in spots with well-worn wooden edges testifying to its popularity.

A brunette waitress flits around, cleavage the only accessory she flaunts. She shoots us a thousand-watt smile, saying in chipper tones, "I'll be right with you, folks."

My eyes settle on the only people in the room, four brutish-looking locals. At least I'd wager they're locals. All appear rugged like the granite of the Sierra Nevada Mountains we drove through to get here.

Two have thick dark hair and beards and the build and attitudes of lumberjacks or maybe mountain men, down to their Carhartt coats and flannel shirts. The other two men are clean-shaven with cowboy hats poised on the table in front of them. At the intersection of cowboys and mountain men, a random question fills my head: Do cowboys ever grow beards? Or mountain men ever wear cowboy hats?

"They don't make men like this in SoCal," I observe, eliciting a frown from Johnny. I mean it sarcastically, but he doesn't get it. He's never had much of a sense of humor with me, especially with things related to other men.

The burly men are mid-cheer, their beer bottles raised in the air and laughing throatily. I'm tempted to order Johnny to start filming because this would make great B-roll footage. But Johnny left his equipment in the van.

The first mountain man I noticed suddenly looks at me,

and a flush of warmth washes over my body. My hand subconsciously goes to the place on my chest where my heart beats as if I'm checking to make sure I still have a pulse. The intense animal magnetism pouring off him lodges a tight knot in my throat.

"Do you need me to wipe the drool off your chin?" Johnny asks morosely. I shake my head, refusing to acknowledge his jealous statement in any other way.

Besides, I've got more pressing matters to attend to ... like letting my eyes crawl over every sexy inch of the mountain man's flesh. Well, what isn't covered by his tan Carhartt coat, flannel, and jeans that is. His gaze returns the favor, sparking a desire so powerful I have to look away, lecturing myself internally to pull it together.

"Very professional, Paige," Johnny needles, placing his arm on my shoulder.

The mountain man's face hardens, though his eyes continue to sear into my skin. I hiss, "And what does that mean?" Stepping forward, I shrug away from Johnny.

He frowns. "If you're going to stand here googly-eyed with the locals, I'm heading back to the bed and breakfast to turn in for the night. You know, we're both adults and can—"

I flip back towards Johnny, glad for an excuse to quit eye fucking the stranger. "I am not sharing a room with you under any circumstances. Sleep in your van." My voice is hard, my proclamation final.

He grimaces, furrowing his brow. "Well, possession is nine-tenths of the law. And I plan on possessing it while you stand here flirting with hicks. So, you can either learn to share or drive to Ophir City."

At my wit's end, I fume. "You made the mess. You sort it out. But that suite is mine, and Phil is going to hear about this." Under any other circumstances, with any other person, the assistant producer would get the room. Johnny's being a total asshole, and I refuse to put up with it. "In the meantime, I want to fill my stomach and get a feel for Military Mountain Man's hometown."

"You mean, get a 'feel' for that guy?" he asks, nodding towards the sexy-as-hell mountain man who continues eyeing me. I look at the toes of my black stilettos, willing the blush to leave my cheeks and my heart to stop pounding. I fail miserably on both counts. My gaze flickers towards the giant of a man. Still staring brazenly at me. Still hotter than fuck. My entire body burns as I soak up the attention, feeling like the only woman in the room despite new patrons arriving and waitresses bustling about.

Johnny rubs his hand over his face, where a pained expression advertises his disapproval. "This is shaping up to be a long fucking night."

I nod, watching the brown-haired, big-breasted waitress approach the table where the mountain man and his three hot companions lurk. I wait for a predictable, lascivious response. If he looks at me—a total stranger—this way, I can only imagine how he treats women beholden to him for a tip. She puts her hand on his large, muscular shoulder, and my stomach knots.

Why the jealous response, Paige? You don't even know this guy. While the last thought is one hundred percent true, it doesn't negate the fact I don't want to share his attention with anyone else.

To my astonishment, the mountain man shrugs off her touch like I did Johnny's, keeping his eyes fixed on me. The corners of his mouth turn up, and I realize he's smiling at me. Not in a creepy or gross kind of way, but as if there's recognition behind the gesture. The way good friends tentatively greet each other after a long absence. Even weirder, my lips mirror his expression. I smile like a freaking schoolgirl. *This* is not good.

"For fuck's sake!" Johnny exclaims next to me as he leads me to an empty table as far away from the men as possible. The move isn't lost on me. But it doesn't deter the mountain man, who cocks his head, twisting to continue taking me in. He clearly doesn't mind being obvious.

My pulse thrums in my temples at his persistence. I'm a big-boned, tall girl at five foot ten. Easily made six feet by my heels. In other words, I'm not the stereotypical, sucked-up skinny Hollywood beauty. So, the affectionate attention is both unexpected and more gratifying than I care to admit. Especially since its source is the hottest guy I've ever seen. Literally a dark-haired version of Liam Hemsworth, only more handsome.

"What?" I ask my camera guy.

Johnny nods towards the man at the table, frowning.

"The locals are friendly," I excuse, my cheeks staining even brighter. I look down bashfully at the dark wood grains of the tabletop before my eyes flutter back towards his. Yep, still looking. Still gorgeous. Still doing crazy things to my heart and body.

"What can I get you two?" the cheery waitress asks, flashing a huge smile at Johnny.

"I can think of a number of things," he replies morosely, crossing his arms as he continues watching me eye the mountain man who brazenly stares back.

"Wanna try the Rough & Ready Red? It's made by a local brewer."

"Since when is this hole-in-the-wall big enough for its own beer label?" Johnny asks, eliciting a grimace from the overly cheerful waitress. I frown, imagining what the prick would say about my hometown.

"It's good," she counters, raising her chin defiantly.

"Whatever," Johnny frowns, leaning back in his chair.

"And you, Miss?" She eyes me curiously, her head bobbing back and forth between the mountain man and me. "Looks like you've caught somebody's eye."

I shake my head, trying to control my damn overheated cheeks. Clearing my throat, I say, "The Rough & Ready Red for me."

"A fan of local brews, then? Nice!" She glares at Johnny to emphasize her point.

"Sure," I explain. "I'm here to immerse myself in this town's vibe."

"And why are you here?" she guardedly asks Johnny.

"Work." His eyes narrow at the poor server, and her face hardens, though she still does her best to maintain the smile painted on her face. "I guess I'll have the same."

"Alright then. I'll be right back with those drinks, and we can talk about apps and entrées."

"You serve food in this dingy joint?" Johnny exaggerates a look of disgust.

The server bites her bottom lip. I can tell she's at her wit's end, and I can't blame her. I wonder how many rude, entitled tourists she deals with daily.

"Yes, we do, and it's good food. We've been featured in *Roadside Dives and Small-Town Eats* twice over the past decade."

"Well, la dee dah." He grimaces, the gesture deepening as he apprises the look of disapproval on my face.

"You've got menus. Take your time deciding while I get your beverages." She heads for the bar, exhaling sharply and shaking her head.

I scold, "It's a small town, Johnny. You'd do well to try being nicer and quit looking down your nose on everyone."

He's always had a chip on his shoulder the size of the Empire State Building, and being in what he refers to as "flyover country" doesn't help one bit.

"Sorry, Paige. I'm not accustomed to rubbing elbows with backwoods folk..."

Like you. He doesn't utter the words, but his countenance says as much.

The bar door swings wide, and the bell clangs as a new man enters Stonie's. My eyes stray to his face. Long, strawberry blond beard, beady eyes, thin face, even thinner lips and a bulbous, puggish nose. My pulse increases.

Is that the same guy who drove me off the road earlier? I can't be certain because everything happened so fast, and he doesn't look in my direction. But there's something eerily familiar about his face, and the fact he won't look at me feels awkward, too. He heads to the bar, perching on a stool with a direct line of sight to me as unease washes over me.

As our waitress passes the table filled with hunks, the mountain man grabs her arm. She leans down, speaking with him. There it is. The flirting I've been expecting. Yet, he continues to eye me as they converse.

Behind the mountain man, the guy seated by the brown cowboy hat with thick black hair, high cheekbones, tan skin, and dreamy eyes jumps up. Heading toward the jukebox, he peruses the songs.

Despite feeling on edge about the blonde bearded man at the bar, I try to convince myself he's a different man. Or if he is the road rager, maybe he doesn't recognize me. I never see the guy look my way, which helps with denial.

Johnny whines, "Just when I thought they couldn't get any less sophisticated."

My eyes jump back to the table of hotties. The other two men at the table lean in, shoving the mountain man's shoulders and nodding in my direction. Suddenly, I feel transported back to a middle school playground with the friends of a cute boy I like, encouraging him to ask me out.

The opening strains of Chris Stapleton's "Whiskey and You" vibrate in the air, and my heart pounds as the tall, dark, and handsome stranger continues staring in my direction and rewarding my return glances with gorgeous grins that highlight his dimpled cheeks.

God should never make men this tempting. Not that I should tell the Divine what to do. But this man is a danger to all womankind. All I can think about is covering those delectable dimples with my lips.

Our server plops two sweating beers on the tabletop, saying, "You have an admirer. Your drinks are covered for the night, as well as anything else you order."

"I'm fucking done," Johnny exclaims, shaking his head and glaring at the guys at the table. He stands unceremoniously, grabbing his beer and heading for the door. "You can cover mine, too, motherfucker," he grumbles as the server looks after him, her mouth gaping.

"What's wrong with him?" she asks, arching an eyebrow.

"You want the full laundry list?" I ask with a laugh.

She shakes her head. I look at her name tag, reading Florence.

"Can I get you anything to eat? Like I said, the gentleman over there's got you covered for the night." She nods towards him, his attention even more raptly on me.

"Is he a good guy?" I ask, my heart pounding in my chest. "A local?"

"Yes, and yes. He's the best," she replies with a slight envious edge to her otherwise cheery voice. "And he's definitely only got eyes for you. That's not something you see every day with him. But then, you don't see him every day, either. He likes to stick to the woods. That's pretty common with a lot of the guys around here."

"And what's his name?" I ask.

She shrugs. "I'll leave introductions to him. Any food?"

"No, thank you. I'm happy with the beer for now."

"Looks like your questions are about to be answered," she warns, and my eyes flash towards the mountain man sauntering towards my table.

Chapter Four

PAIGE

My eyes meet those of the burly man standing in front of me, another adorable, lopsided grin on his face that hints at the dimples beneath the beard. His warm eyes wash over me, and I'm thoroughly glad I'm sitting because my knees feel weak. *What in the hell is wrong with me?*

"Hey," he says in a voice equal parts gruff and bashful. I'm not used to seeing a big brute of a man so timid. It captivates me.

"Hi," I reply quietly, inadvertently reflecting his introverted energy with a hefty dose of awkward single woman who can't remember the last time she got laid.

He clears his throat, swallowing loudly and furrowing his brows. "You want to dance?"

An uncontrollable smile captures my lips. "I've barely been in town two hours. Are you locals always this forward?"

He pauses, his eyes still captivating mine as he thinks through the question before confessing, "I'm never like this."

I knit my forehead, breath picking up speed. "Oh, yeah? Decided to turn over a new leaf, then?"

His smile grows larger. "Nope, but I had to at least ask."

"Why?"

"Because you're definitely not something I could pass up without regretting it for a long, long time."

My brain races to think up something flirty to say in return. "Sounds more like a case of FOMO to me."

"No, ma'am." He shakes his head, stepping towards me, a question on his face.

I nod, and he offers me his hand, pulling me to my feet and loosely into his arms. He leads me towards the jukebox and the lone pool table, where an empty space begs for dancing.

"You don't know me yet," he says as though that fact is about to change forever. "But I don't do regret. Or FOMO, for that matter."

"Good thing," I answer, flirtation coloring my voice. "Because I don't either."

"Who's the guy you came in with? He kept staring daggers at me."

I exhale, shaking my head. "Someone who always oversteps his boundaries."

The man's thick dark brown brows furrow, and his mahogany eyes drill into me. "Boyfriend? Lover? Husband?" He steals a look at my left hand and empty ring finger with the last question, letting out an audible exhale.

"Employee." It's a slight simplification, but whatever.

His face relaxes.

"And I never mix business with pleasure." I melt in the stranger's strong, warm embrace, uncertain of what it is about him that puts me at immediate ease. But after the day I've had, I thirst for this feeling.

My eyes glance back towards the bar, noticing the man who came in earlier has disappeared. *Thank God!* A small part of me wonders if dancing with this giant has scared him away.

The thought fills me with gratitude and makes me feel down-right clingy. Like I never want to let him go.

"It's a good thing we don't work together then."

"Oh, yeah? Why's that?"

"Because I believe rules are made to be broken."

"Oh, really?" I smile, unrepentantly returning his heated gaze.

"What's your name?" the handsome man asks, his eyes continuing to drill into me.

"No offense, but I don't do names with strangers."

"Well, what do I call you, then? Woman?" He creases his forehead.

I laugh, unable to deny the practicality of some kind of naming convention. "My middle name's Annalise."

"Middle names? Really?"

I nod, adding, "Look, I'm just passing through. Which means there's no reason to use real names."

"Boy, you have a way of putting things into shitty perspective."

"It's one of my strengths." I agree with a smile. "For a man who wants to know so much about me, you have yet to share. What's your name?"

"You mean my middle name?"

"Now you're catching on."

"Ansel."

The jukebox goes silent for a moment before the cowboy with the brown hat starts another song, looking in our direction with a pleased grin. Luke Combs's "Forever After All."

"Wow," I say, shaking my head.

"What?" the mountain man murmurs, wrapping his arms ever so slightly tighter around my waist. One more inch and my soft core will be pressed against his hard, muscular one. The thought makes my head spin and awakens the juncture between my legs.

My voice sounds oddly breathless as I answer, "Your wingmen are working overtime."

He chuckles, his face a heady mixture of handsome and covetous, as if he's staring at a precious, one-of-a-kind treasure. "They're my brothers," he excuses, and I eye them again. They all look around the same age and share no family resemblance. He must read the question in my eyes because he adds, "Foster brothers if you want to get technical."

"Oh," I whimper, my voice failing me in ways it hasn't since high school. "I forgot to check your left hand, Ansel. Where's your wife tonight?" I say it flirtatiously but also to make sure. Besides mixing business with pleasure, I never cheat. And everything about this man, from his breathtaking face to his firm, large body and foresty, clean smell, indicates he can't possibly be single.

"Right here, if fate gives me a say in the matter."

His words floor me, and I struggle to respire, let alone speak. Taking a deep breath, I manage in jaded tones, "Just when I thought pickup lines couldn't get any cheesier. But it's also my fault. I kind of walked into that one."

"It's not a pickup line, it's the goddamned truth."

"Okay," I say with a frown, thoroughly unconvinced and highly aware he hasn't answered my question. Convenient. "Let me put it another way. Who are you trying to cheat on tonight?" I arch my eyebrow.

"Cheat?" He scrunches his face, shaking his head. "No, ma'am. I may be a lot of things—anti-social, rough around the edges, crude at times. But I'm no cheater. Never have been. Never will be."

"Good," I nod. "We see eye to eye on that."

"I had a girl once," he adds, as if further qualifying his previous statement. "Who cheated on me while I was in Afghan. So, yeah, I know how that feels, and it sucks. I would never do that to anyone."

"Afghanistan?"

"I'm a Marine."

"Oh."

"Former Marine if you want to get technical."

"Wait," I counter, staring into his warm chocolaty eyes. "Isn't it once a Marine, always a Marine?"

"Semper Fi. I just don't want you thinking I'm going to leave you high and dry anytime soon."

"Anytime soon?"

"Or maybe ever," he adds as we sway around the limited space. Another song comes on, "Tonight Looks Good on You," by Jason Aldean.

"I love this song," I say, grinning up at the big brute of a man. "And this goes without saying, but your brothers really are going above and beyond to help you out." I glance in their direction. The cowboy at the jukebox has returned to the table to retrieve his brown Stetson, and the other two stand, preparing to leave. "Oops, I spoke too soon. Looks like your entourage is leaving. I should let you go."

The three men nod in our direction, and Ansel returns the gesture before they head for the door.

"No, ma'am. I'm right where I belong."

"Are you now?"

He nods firmly.

"They seemed like they were in a rush all of a sudden," I observe, feeling oddly nervous even as the front door of the bar keeps swinging and more people pour in.

"They've all got women to get home to." A hint of loneliness colors his voice at the end. I know exactly how he feels.

"I still don't buy that you're single," I say with a grin, shaking my head and looking up at the massive man. "I don't mean to objectify you, but you're pretty damn hot."

"Objectify me all you want. I'm fine with it."

I shake my head, annoyed at the heat on my cheeks.

"Who's going to man the jukebox now that they're gone?" I tease, trying to lighten the mood.

He shrugs, never taking his eyes off me.

Clearing my throat, I try to make a little conversation, cool down the fiery electricity sizzling back and forth between us. "So, why were your brothers so intent on matchmaking tonight?" I ask, unable to avoid the obvious.

Ansel laughs. "It's more like they had a running bet to see how long it'd take for me to say something stupid and fuck this up."

"Stupid? I wouldn't go that far. But brash? Yes."

"And you're still in my arms."

"I am. Aren't I?" I scrunch my nose.

"You're adorable when you do that."

"Do what? Look at you like one or the other of us is crazy?"

"Is that what that look means?" he asks, leaning closer and burying his head lightly in my hair. "Maybe we both are," he adds in low tones.

"Maybe."

"I like the way you smell."

"I could say the same about you," I reply.

He continues, "Your perfume is citrusy with a hint of vanilla. Like one of those orange popsicles with the cream in the center."

I can't help the giggle that escapes my lips. "Well, you're definitely no poet."

"I'm honest and straightforward. You always know what you get with me. Isn't that a good thing?"

"Generally, yes. But I'm suspending judgment when it comes to you."

"Suspending judgment? How is that fair? You've already got me hook, line, and sinker."

"That's how fools are born, Ansel," I remind.

"Maybe," he agrees, wrapping his arms more tightly around my waist and unrepentantly pressing me against his firm core. The move is satisfying in ways I can't begin to express while simultaneously sinking me deeper into the ravenous mire of desire entangling us.

What in the hell is my problem? All I know with any certainty is that Ansel makes me feel safer than any man ever has. It's exactly what I need right now.

"Ansel and Annalise. You don't hear those two names every day, yet somehow they go together. Don't you think?"

I shake my head, chuckling. "No wonder your brothers are betting against you. Haven't you ever heard of taking things slow?"

He shrugs. "That's overrated. Especially when you spend most of your time in the Sierra backcountry."

"In the backcountry? You really are a mountain man, then?" I ask incredulously, fingering his flannel shirt and staring at his beard.

He laughs heartily. "A mountain man? I don't know. I guess you could call me that. I mean, I do live in the forest, and I make my living as an outfitter."

"An outfitter? Like of clothes?"

He chuckles some more, his chest rumbling and filling my body with delicious waves of deep vibration. "I guide hunting and fishing trips. Everything from logistics and management to environmental stewardship."

"You make it sound so nice," I say with a snort.

"What?"

"Stalking and killing animals that have done nothing to you."

"Don't tell me you're one of those vegan PETA girls," he stops dancing, staring at me with a frown.

"And what if I am?" I raise my chin in challenge, taking immediate offense to his comment.

41

"Then, I'm fucked."

"How so?" I arch my eyebrow.

"Because what you do to my heart isn't right or probably even legal ... whether or not you're one of those hippy-dippy, tie-herself-to-a-tree kinds of girls."

"I can think of worse ways to make a stand."

"So, you are, then?" he laments.

I snicker. "Well, honestly, you could call me more of a pescatarian. But that doesn't mean I don't see great value in protecting the environment."

"A pesca... what?" His forehead creases. He couldn't get any cuter, working his scowl overtime—somehow simultaneously sexy as hell and disarmingly boyish.

"Pescatarian."

"What does that mean exactly?"

"I'm mostly vegetarian, although I will occasionally eat fish."

He sighs, his face relaxing. "Well, that's a relief. Fishing around here's plentiful. I'm constantly pulling beautiful Kokanee salmon out of the creek behind my cabin. You'd be willing to eat that, right?"

"As long as it has gills, scales, and fins, I'm okay with it. Oh, and it has to be ethically and sustainably sourced."

"Always. I don't do anything unless it's sportsman-like. You know, I care very much about environmental stewardship, too. Most hunters do. After all, we have a vested interest in keeping the land pristine and wildlife healthy."

I shake my head, confused. "But wait a second. How does shooting innocent animals square with that?"

"First of all, there's no such thing as guilty or innocent animals. Nature operates under a different code than human beings. Period. It's not right or wrong. It just is, no matter how we try to anthropomorphize nature."

"So, you're trying to tell me Bambi and Thumper don't really exist?"

"No, I'm trying to tell you that under the right circumstances, Bambi would tear you to shreds with its hooves and antlers, and Thumper would bite and claw you to bits. The bottom line with nature is survival ... *at all costs*. There's no margin for error, and second chances are rarely given."

"And somehow you find that comforting?" I ask, knitting my forehead.

"Yeah, because I know exactly what to expect. What to anticipate. I find people and social situations much harder to read than the laws of nature."

"You're doing alright with me," I reply, shrugging.

"Am I really? You keep saying that I'm taking things too fast. But I don't know how else to do it with you."

"You mean with women in general?" I correct.

"No, I mean with you specifically."

"And why is that?" I ask, my heart pounding in my chest and my inner voice chastising me for asking. I'm fully conscious of where this line of questioning will lead, and there's a dangerous part of me that welcomes it. *Am I really that easily swayed by a handsome face?*

He leans closer, whispering against the shell of my ear. "Every eye in this room is on you and me. How about we give them something to talk about?"

"Haven't we already? "

He shakes his head.

Clearing my throat, I squeak. "And what do you have in mind, Stranger?"

Chapter Five

RIDGE

"And what do you have in mind, Stranger?"

Did she really just ask me that? Bringing my hand up to her cheek, I push back a stray hair, running my pointer finger sensually along her jawline to her rounded chin. Snagging my finger there, I push her head up, encouraging Annalise to look me in the eyes. When they meet mine, her defenses drop a tick. Just enough to urge me towards her until I can feel her warm breath on my lips.

We're so close I can almost taste her. But I stop short, needing her to close the minuscule gap between us. Show me she's as into this as I am. Hell, I'm verging on pathetic with the way I keep coming onto her, but true beauty does strange things to a man ... even a wild one who prefers evergreens and alpine streams to most social situations.

Her dark, velvety eyes tick to my lips. It's all I need. My resolve to wait crumbles as I lean slightly forward, enough for our lips to touch in the breathy space between want and desire. A sexy little sigh, almost inaudible, escapes her lips, and my heart pounds in my chest. Lust snakes through my body like the water-choked streams of Rough & Ready Country when the snowmelt begins, even as our lips simmer and burn with wanton energy.

My chest rumbles with satisfaction as I angle my head to the side, pressing her more firmly into me and letting my lips gently tease and dance over hers. Playfully, I encourage her to relax, enjoy, and maybe even savor this delicious moment.

She dissolves in my arms, her respiration increasing. Her lips grow more supple and demanding, wresting fiery sparks of yearning from deep within my core. Annalise sighs softly, and I can't help myself, dropping my head a little more and sweeping possessively into her mouth.

Her hands clasp the back of my neck, drawing my face against hers, my lips stinging with heightened passion and pressure. The warm silkiness of her gifted tongue circles and swirls mine, centering all thoughts and focus on making this woman mine. Showing her through my touch and lips that I'm enough to keep her fully and completely satisfied.

She starts to pull back, but not enough to deter me. My palms slide up her shoulders, past her fragile collarbones and long neck, to grasp her cheeks and steady her head. I change the angle of mine slightly, letting me go deeper. She whimpers against my lips, a delicate yet heady sound that makes blood rush to the cock pressed firmly against her stomach.

Fuck, I've got to get myself under control. I may want to devour her right here, but I'm also a gentleman. Even years spent in the wilderness haven't been able to beat my pop, Wyatt's chivalrous training out of me. And I want this woman to know I have far greater designs for her than sex. Even though the mere thought of it knots up my insides and undoes me all at once.

Pulling back, I smile bashfully.

Her eyebrows arch, and her cheeks darken as her eyes snap around the room. "You're right. It seems all eyes *are* on us."

I nod, not giving two fucks about anybody else but the beauty in front of me.

"I guess we're the best action that can be expected in a town that rolls up Main Street around ten," she observes.

I chuckle, wrapping my arm around her waist and leading her towards the table my brothers recently vacated. Pulling out a chair for her, she sits, and I gently push her in. I sit across from her, noticing Annalise's hand come up to rest on the table. I can't help myself, greedily grabbing it and threading my fingers with hers. Her eyes tick to our hands, her cheeks outright glowing as she giggles. "You really are over the top, aren't you?"

"Is it too much?" Those are the four hardest words I've ever muttered. But I'm fully aware of how overwhelming I can be with women I'm attracted to. It hardly ever happens and never this strongly, though, which has me wrestling to maintain control and not look desperate.

She shakes her head, her eyes dropping to the empty table top recently bussed to remove the empty beer bottles left by me and my brothers.

"So, I know your middle name and that you're not from around here. And I know you're a pesca... What was that again?"

"A pescatarian."

I nod, determined to sear the term into my brain. "But there's so much I have yet to learn about you. Like why you're visiting Hollister?"

Annalise shrugs, her fingers actively caressing mine and teasing over my rough palm. Her touch is soft, flirtatious, and so captivating I swallow loudly, trying to keep my head on straight. If a gesture this innocent drives me wild, what in the hell could this woman do to me if she actually put her mind to it?

"Here for work."

"Oh, yes, that's right. I almost forgot about your employee earlier. He sure didn't seem to like us together."

The corners of her mouth turn down. "He's harmless. But he can get oddly jealous for a colleague."

"Did you used to date or anything?"

"Briefly. It was a terrible mistake." Her voice rings with a conviction that I lap up like a stray cat in a milking barn. The state of this woman's availability shouldn't intrigue me so much, but I can't help myself. She's got my insides simultaneously swarming with lust, jealousy, and an overwhelming need to protect her. It's almost too much. The kind of emotional override that usually shuts me down.

But getting to know this unconvinced visitor, maybe even make her see the sparks flying between us are worth exploring, pushes me well past my comfort zone. Annalise is already healing my intimacy issues, and I barely know her. I wonder what the promise of an actual relationship might look like with her.

"What's that far-off stare for?" she asks, calling me back to the present.

I grin, and her eyes dart to my cheeks. "What? Do I have something on my face?"

She chuckles. "No. It's just your dimples."

"My dimples?" I furrow my brows.

"Yeah, they're drool-worthy."

Her words make me feel invincible. "I guess it's only fair, considering every inch of you is pretty damn drool-worthy, too."

"I saw the waitress flirting with you earlier. What's the deal? An old flame?" A tinge of jealousy colors her voice.

"You mean Florence? Hell, no! We went to the same middle and high school, although she's a few years younger than me. She feels more like a little sister than anything."

"She doesn't seem to see things that way," Annalise

47

observes, frowning as the brunette server heads our way. She's lost her cheery voice and fake smile, trading it for disgruntled glances in Annalise's direction.

"What else can I get you two?"

I look at the beauty whose hand I still hold quizzically. "Another beer? And maybe something to eat?" I start to suggest Stonie's delish sliders before remembering what the woman said about being a pescatarian. "They do a decent fish and chips. Does that sound good to you?"

"Wow, I didn't realize how hungry I am until your suggestion. My stomach literally lurched. Fish and chips sound amazing, and, yes, I'd love another beer."

I wasn't expecting the buttoned-up, professional woman to say yes. Her answer fortifies what I already know. Something unique and special is happening between us.

I have to scream my order, annoyance gripping me as more and more people pour in, and the place gets downright deafening. I expect Annalise to be okay with the amassing crowd. But when I shoot another look in her direction, she stares blankly ahead at the multiplying crowd, obviously uncomfortable. To top things off, the jukebox goes from the country love songs my brother Hawk kept feeding it to something like death metal. Loud, brazen, and impossible to hold a conversation over.

Leaning towards her, mere inches from her ear, I scream to be heard above the din of the room. We've worn out our welcome here, but I'm afraid if I propose relocating, she'll use it as an excuse to bail on me altogether. And the sharp ache in my chest lets me know I'm not ready to let this woman go.

"You okay?" I ask.

She nods, smiling wanly. "It's getting a little loud and kind of hot in here, don't you think?

"Yeah." I'm heartened that we agree.

"And the music," she laments, covering her ears with her hands.

I nod, knowing my voice can't compete with the growling lyrics and lavish guitar and drum solos.

Her eyes tick to my teeth, rounding, and she covers her mouth with her hand. Scrutinizing her more closely, trying to figure out what she's laughing at, I notice her white blouse glows in the overhead blacklight. She giggles some more, and I realize her upper right canine is glowing in the light, which inspires my own chuckle.

Leaning into me and setting my blood on fire, she whispers so close to the shell of my ear that I feel her lips feathering over it. "Your front tooth looks dark in the blacklight. Like it's missing."

Oh, shit. The lighting in the bar's given away my dental implant. But I can't feel especially self-conscious with the way her shirt and canine glow back at me.

"Look at your shirt..."

She looks down, holding out her arms and laughing some more.

"And no offense, but your tooth is glowing."

She gasps, slapping her hand over her mouth. Her face is awash in embarrassment as she explains, "I have a crown thanks to high school softball."

"What'd you take a ball to the face or something?"

"Thankfully, no. But I was playing first base when a rival player decided to turn the game into a very violent contact sport."

"Ouch."

"How about you?" she asks, gesturing towards my mouth.

"Fake tooth. High school basketball," I say with a shrug.

"You don't need to say anymore," she says, still eyeing my smile wildly and laughing. "You know, I would never know if it wasn't for the silly lighting."

"Too bad we don't have one of those old velvet Sublime posters. You ever seen one of those under blacklight?"

"Of course. My mom and dad were way into Sublime. And other bands like Cypress Hill, Phish, and, of course, the Dead."

"Sounds like you were raised by stoners." I go out on a limb.

Annalise nods. "More or less. But I'd definitely say their lack of ambition encouraged me to take a different route in life if that makes sense?"

"Believe me, it does. As a foster kid, the only place I could go was up. Fortunately, I was lucky enough to get an old, polite, stern cowboy for a foster dad and fourteen pain-in-the-ass brothers who are like my best friends."

"I could tell they really love you, and they acted very supportive, maybe overly supportive as your wingmen."

"Well, they know better than anyone that I'm picky as hell, and it isn't often I find something I'm interested in." We both have to scream at each other, which makes this intriguing conversation simultaneously exhausting.

"So, when you find that something, you go all-in immediately?"

"Overwhelmed much?" I ask, feeling called out.

A busboy interrupts our conversation, placing two big baskets of steaming fish and chips on the table in front of us. Florence stands behind him with two beers. One look at Annalise tells me exactly what I need to do. "Sorry to ask this, Florence. But would you mind boxing these up for us? It's gotten a little loud in here for our tastes."

"Sure thing." I rifle in my back pocket, pull out my wallet, and hand her my debit card. "Make sure you treat yourself well," I say with a wink that resurrects her smile.

As soon as Annalise and I get outside, holding our to-go boxes and beers, I breathe a sigh of relief. She echoes my gesture, a warm glow making her symmetrical face even more lovely. Heading towards my truck, her strides slow, shrinking the nearer we get.

"You're not planning on driving after drinking..."

"God, no," I reply, shaking my head emphatically. "I may be a country boy, but I'm no idiot. That said, I've got a few blankets we can throw in the bed to make things comfortable while we eat and scope out the stars. Sound like a plan?"

"Away from the crowds and the loud music? Absolutely!" She looks up, her jaw dropping to the ground. "Wow! I've never seen anything like this. Not even in Yosemite."

My eyes follow hers, taking in the pristine nighttime sky scattered haphazardly with sparkling diamonds. "Too bad we still have to deal with Hollister's streetlights. If we were out at my place, you'd be truly amazed. You can see the Milky Way in all its glory." These are sights I take for granted, but as Annalise soaks up the beauty of the moment, I live vicariously through her, remembering my first time seeing a sky like this.

"I came to live here a couple of months after my tenth birthday, and I remember looking up at night for the first time. It made my jaw drop, too." I shrug, chuckling. "And then, I guess I got used to it."

"Got used to this? How is that possible?"

I cock my head to the side, soaking up the way she marvels at the universe. This will never get old to me: her oval face filled with awe, her plump, tasty lips parted, her eyes wide and greedily trying to soak up the stellar visual.

As she continues staring heavenward, letting her ravenous gaze wash over the firmament, I unlock my truck cab, retrieving the blankets I have in the cab and piling them into the truck bed. I've got a raised, silver Chevy dually, so I have to boost the tall, black-haired beauty into the back before handing her our to-go boxes and brews and piling in behind her.

"Aren't we violating some open container law?" she asks, finally pulling her gaze away from the astrological spectacle glittering above us.

"More than likely," I reply, drawing as close to her as possible without seeming creepy. "But my brother's the sheriff of Gold County. So, if need be, I'll call in a favor."

"You do that a lot?" She arches her eyebrow.

I'm not sure if she means her last sentence as a statement or a question, but I go the second route, feeling a strange need to explain myself. "Never, actually. That's why I figure I could just this once. Besides, this is not enough to get me drunk. And even when I do get a little saucy, I've never been the bois-terous type. You know, out looking for trouble and attention."

"Is that what made you choose to live in the woods? A general disinterest in trouble and attention?" I watch her dive into her fish and chips, closing her eyes and letting out a satis-fied puff of air as she takes her first bite of the crispy, golden-battered fish. Her obvious pleasure envelops my heart in warmth. If I'm not careful, I could get addicted to making her happy.

"Good?"

"Mmhmm..." she answers, still chewing. But I can tell by the sated look on her face that she approves. It reminds me of the look that lit up her face after our kiss in front of the jukebox.

"Not bad for a dive bar in the middle of nowhere, right?"

She nods emphatically, still chewing. After a few moments, she adds, "Not bad at all. I've got a foodie friend who travels the country, profiling small venues off the beaten path. I'm going to tell her about this place."

I nod, trying not to let my eyes rest too long on her face. But it's an impossible task. I have the odd impression I could stare at her all night without growing tired or bored. But I'm not going for creepy or awkward, so I pull my eyes away.

Opening my takeout box, I dive in. As usual, the fish is crispy and savory and the French fries done to perfection. "You know, this town's actually known for its local eats. Stonie's isn't even the best spot. There's Sweet Rush in the morning for baked goods and ice cream in the afternoons during the summer months, and the Silver Fork used to have the best lunch and dinner menu, especially the Black Forest cake. It was sinful perfection." *Sinful perfection? Like Annalise.*

"Why past tense? Did the place close?"

I nod, not sure what to say. "Yeah, the owner, Jerry, skipped out of town after Christmas, and the place has sat vacant ever since. It's kind of the town mystery."

"Hmm... That's some juicy small-town drama."

"This place is filled with drama," I chuckle. "Because we all know each other so well that one man or woman's problem is everyone's problem. And people also feel extra generous with advice. I suppose it's like that in all small towns."

"I think so. I grew up in Valley Springs."

"Valley Springs? That's even smaller than Hollister."

She chuckles, leaning towards me just enough so our shoulders playfully brush. The innocent move sends my pulse into overdrive. "Last time I checked, the town was just under a thousand residents."

"I'm surprised. You come off as a sophisticated, big-city girl at first glance."

She shrugs. "Work keeps me close to the city."

"The City?" I ask, referring to San Francisco.

She smiles enigmatically. "Why spoil tonight with work talk? I'd much rather discuss the places I like to visit, like Yosemite and Mount Whitney."

"Both fantastic locations, although the crowds at Yosemite overwhelm me."

"Me, too."

Clearing my throat, I ask, "You more or less know what I do for a living. How about yourself?"

The corners of her mouth turn down. "Career-wise, I'm kind of in transition at the moment."

"And why's that?"

She looks up to the right in thought, licking her lips. "A long story that I don't feel like diving into right now. I try to save work talk for the office. But suffice it to say, I make a living telling other people's stories."

"You mean, like a writer?"

"Kind of," she says with a nod. Her continued vagueness stokes my curiosity. But I can tell she has trust issues. So, I bite my tongue, letting further questions go and waiting for her to open up to me in her own time and her own way.

Chapter Six

PAIGE

"The small-town hunting guide and the big-city storyteller? It's an odd mix."

"Indeed," the burly mountain man next to me agrees. I can't get over how handsome he is as my eyes try to sear his visual memory into my brain. He is definitely the most delectable guy I've ever met. Too bad they don't make men like him in SoCal. The thought brings my mind back to Johnny—the last person in the world I want to think about right now. Stiffening, I wonder if he's already tried to take over the B&B suite. If so, there's going to be hell to pay.

"What's that look for?" Ansel asks, his dark eyes penetrating me.

I shrug. "Just worrying about later when I have to return to the bed and breakfast where I'm staying tonight."

"Mrs. Chatterton's place?"

"It's the only place we could find in town. But my employee messed up the room booking, so we only have one room for the both of us."

Ansel's face hardens, his jaw tightening and his muscles

rippling beneath the beard. "And you think that was a mistake?"

"I don't know," I reply, grabbing another French fry to absentmindedly crunch on. "That said, I made it very clear he would have to find accommodations elsewhere or sleep in his van. And I took the room key. But I'm not looking forward to going back over there to see what he ultimately decided to do. After all, I'm sure he could easily talk Mrs. Chatterton into another room key."

"I'll go with you," Ansel says firmly, and my eyebrows jump into my hairline.

"Oh, no. You don't have to do that. I wasn't telling you any of this to get your help. I was simply answering the question you asked about what was bothering me."

"He acted jealous as fuck earlier. And the way he glared at me was unsettling. You need to be on guard around him."

"Is that your sixth sense speaking?"

"Yes, ma'am. I was a Marine Scout Sniper. I had to rely on my read of people constantly, making life-or-death decisions in the blink of an eye. Overwatch made me both a guardian angel and an angel of death."

"That's an odd dichotomy," I observe.

He nods.

"So, you went from hunting people to hunting animals?"

"If you want to make me sound like a psychopath, I guess you could put it that way." He grimaces. "But I'd prefer to say I went from serving my country to serving outdoorsmen."

"That does have a nicer ring to it."

"No Marine ever died on my overwatch. That's why I did what I did. To keep my comrades safe ... to make sure they returned home to their families in one piece."

"That's a lot of responsibility for one man," I say, really looking at him. His gaze makes my insides feel as hot and melty as chocolate chip cookies fresh from the oven. And I catch flickers of lighter cinnamon and amber in his eyes, enhancing their soulful depth.

"The Corps usually works us in teams of two. So, the responsibility was shared."

I don't feel any less awestruck as I stare up at him through the thick fringe of my black eyelashes.

"You know, I like it better out here for so many reasons," the mountain man says, his face flickering back towards Stonie's. "But I don't feel I got to dance with you for nearly as long as I wanted to. What say we give it another whirl? After we finish our food and beers."

I rub my stomach, already feeling full. "I don't know how much more I can eat, but I don't really feel like going back inside."

"We don't have to go back inside," he says, grinning until the skin around his eyes crinkles. "How old are you, Annalise?"

My face registers surprise. "That question just came out of nowhere."

"Yeah, it kind of did, didn't it?"

"Thirty-two. And you?"

"Thirty-four. I guess this is about the time I should ask you how you feel about older men..."

I laugh. "Back to not playing it cool, I see. The thing is, I don't do long-distance relationships, so there's really no point in having this conversation."

"No point?" he asks with a dark laugh. "You're at least U.S.-based, right?"

"California-based, if you want to get technical."

"Then what's the problem?"

"California's a big state."

"Even if you're north of Eureka or south of San Diego, that's nothing compared to what long distance meant when I was in the service."

I shrug, my heart inexplicably pounding in my chest and making it increasingly difficult to act unaffected. "I don't know."

He cocks his head to the side. "If you're not feeling this, no problem. I get it, and I'm sorry I wasted your time." He closes his unfinished to-go box as if punctuating the statement.

"It's not that I'm not feeling it. It's that I see the impossibility of the whole thing."

"I guess you and I have very different definitions of impossible."

"Perhaps," I say with a shrug. "I didn't mean to give you the wrong impression. I really, really have enjoyed everything about tonight, and I don't want it to end. But seeing as the writing's already on the wall, it's hard not to envision that ending."

"I understand," he says, steeling his voice. His eyes sear into mine, making my throat tighten and my breath come faster.

"And I have an appointment tomorrow. So, I shouldn't be out much later because mornings are hard enough without being sleep-deprived."

He says gruffly, drawing closer to me and making my pulse pound in my temples, "See, I'd let things go between us. Wish you a good night and be done with this impromptu date. But your body keeps telling me a different story than your tongue."

"Oh?" I say, knitting my brows.

"Yeah. Your eyes are all warm and dilated, swirling with something like desire. And you keep licking your lips and running your fingers through your hair. You know, telltale signs of attraction. And then, between the flare of your nostrils, the pulse point flickering in your neck, and the way your eyes like to settle on my mouth,

58

I'd wager we're on the same page feelings-wise. Am I wrong?"

His mouth hovers two inches from mine, and I'm certain he can hear my heart jackhammering against my ribs. *For God's sake, what's wrong with me?* His warm, large hand comes up, tucking the hair behind my ear, and his eyes flicker to my mouth. But he doesn't move apart from the fingertips that glide sensually and lightly over my cheek.

I swallow loudly, clearing my throat. "I know what I keep saying," I confess softly. "But I'm not ready to go back to the room yet, and I'm not sure I could sleep even if I did. So, how about we call a truce when it comes to future talk and enjoy being in the moment?" The last word comes out breathlessly.

"Deal," he says, leaning back against the cab of his truck and looking up skyward. Talk about a tease.

After a long, tense silence where I attempt to marvel at the wonders of the night sky rather than think about all the ways I want this mountain man to possess and violate me, the burly man points upwards, asking, "You see that cluster of stars that looks like a bowl and stem?"

"You mean the Big Dipper?"

"Yes, Ursa Major. If you take the two outer stars in the bowl, they point to Polaris or the North Star. That way, you'll always know where you're going."

"I wish it was that simple," I grumble, fully aware that he's talking in realities while I'm speaking in metaphors.

He side-eyes me somberly. "Sometimes, knowing where you're going is more difficult than it sounds, especially when you have to rely on others to get there."

"Oh, I try never to rely on anybody," I reply quickly without thinking.

"We all have to rely on others, Annalise. Thinking you don't have to is an illusion."

I frown, unable to argue with him.

"Nevertheless, it's worth asking why you feel you can't rely on others."

I shrug. "Because it's a surefire way to get let down."

"It can be. What has your experience been with getting let down?"

"I guess it started with my parents. I think you've already figured out they were both potheads. No motivation, nothing really beyond smoking weed and making just enough money to squeak by. And I mean, squeak. But I'm not made like them. I want more from life, and I don't want to settle for poverty, worry, and a perpetual lack of abundance because I'm lazy and lacking in ambition. I suppose I shouldn't talk about my parents that way, but it's the truth. And they don't think much of me, accusing me of being a capitalist, a workaholic, and just another cog in the machine. Maybe I am, but I'd like to think I'm a cog making a difference."

He nods, listening intently, his hands folded in his lap. "I can't imagine you not making a difference in this world, Annalise. You're the most captivating, strong, engaging woman I've ever met. But returning to your parents, accurately assessing their faults doesn't mean you don't love them. I firmly believe we're supposed to learn from the good and bad of our parents."

"And what have you learned from yours and your time as a foster kid?"

He scratches his head, his face serious for a moment. "If you had asked me that even three or four years ago, I'd have told you how much my parents sucked for what they did to me and how much I resented them. But the older I get, the more I realize they had a full deck of problems they were dealing with, though many self-imposed. The guy I believe was my father was a lot older than my mom ... a good thirty years or more. He was wealthy and owned a lot of property in Bakersfield. His money pulled my mom in, your classic gold digger. I mean, we're talking a stripper who used her looks to exploit and take advantage of countless men. So, when my father showed up, she married him in a whirlwind and then proceeded to take everything the old man was worth."

"Oh, wow..." Silence greets us as I watch the muscle working in his jaw.

"Mom was into drugs, and the sudden influx of disposable cash was the worst possible thing for her. And the man she married, the guy who I guess was my father, had his doubts about my paternity. Rightfully so, God rest my mother's soul. So, after she died of an overdose, the old man wrote me off. My grandparents on his side were already dead, and my maternal grandparents had disowned Mom a long time ago—well before I came on the scene. She didn't have any siblings, and if my father did, I don't know about them. To top things off, I was an only child. So without next of kin to fall back on, I ended up here."

"You've been through a lot," I remark, straining to digest everything he tells me.

He eyes me stony-faced. "I don't know about that. No one ever really laid a hand on me. Hell, I actually wanted someone to spank or discipline me. Show me some attention. Any attention at all. Believe me, some of my foster brothers went through way worse ... physical abuse, sexual abuse, emotional abuse. I was just straight-up neglected."

I counter, thinking back to the psychology class I took as one of my college prerequisites. "But psychologists say neglect can be the worst kind of abuse because it affects the way you attach and bond with people."

He shrugs, his face ambivalent. "I suppose that would explain my dating history and why I prefer the company of trees and rocks to most people. But I'm well bonded with my brothers, and my dad, Wyatt, is the best father figure a kid could ever ask for. Not that he didn't put us all through it.

61

Learning to rope and ride, wrestle calves and steers, and spend months at a time on the range. I will say the balance of all I've experienced has made me very independent. Another thing I feel like we have in common."

Without reflecting, I grab his hand, squeezing it. His smile is equal parts heated and surprised, and I return a tentative grin, not exactly sure what's come over me. But it feels like somehow there's an understanding between us. As if down to our cores, in our deepest parts, we get each other.

"My parents neglected me, too. It made me highly reactive. Always looking for a way to get their attention. For me, that meant perfect grades and never getting in trouble. Always doing everything pathologically right. But it never worked."

He turns towards me, directing the intensity of his listening gaze in my direction. "It almost sounds like you had it worse than me. At least I was out of my bad circumstances and on the ranch by ten."

I nod, fighting a sudden sting in the back of my eyes. It's not like I haven't discussed this with others before, so I don't know why it makes me suddenly feel dangerously emotional. Maybe it's because I'm not used to being so heard by another human being. I turn towards him a little more, and he brings his free hand up to rest on my hip, lightly stroking it and making it difficult to breathe.

"Yeah, I tried so hard to please them, and they didn't even show up to my high school graduation, though I was the vale-dictorian. And the same with college, although by then, I traded trying to get their attention for chasing all the wrong guys. Always the wrong guys."

"Why the wrong guys?" he asks, his voice soft and empathetic.

"Because looking back, I now realize they were never really that into me. I understand the psychology behind it and every-thing, but there was still something so tempting about trying to win over a person who basically ignored me ... like my parents."

"I went for girls a lot like my mom. Frivolous, superficial, unfaithful, after me for all the wrong reasons. And I suppose I enjoyed the thrill of the chase, too," he says, looking down at our entwined hands.

"Do you think you'll ever get past the adrenaline rush of the hunt?" I ask the question as much for myself as for him.

"I thought I already had until I met you."

Chapter Seven

PAIGE

"I thought I already had until I met you."

His answer catches me off guard, and I snicker nervously, lightly swatting at his shoulder with my free hand. I'm greeted by rock-hard muscles that make my fingertips sting. Grimacing and waving my hand in the air, I ask, "What does that mean?"

"Well, I've been chasing you all night ... rather blatantly."

"You have," I smile, drawing closer to him. The smell of whatever forest-scented soap he uses draws me in like bees to honey. "And I'm not running, although I should."

"Why should you?" he asks, tracing lazy circles with his fingertips on my hip and the outside of my upper thigh and setting my blood on fire.

"Well, for one, because we barely know each other."

"Barely knowing each other and not knowing each other for long are two completely different things. Yes, our timeline is condensed. But I've told you more about myself than most people know. And I imagine you've done the same..."

I nod. "I don't know why, though." I look down, unable to meet his gaze.

"I know why on my end."

"Why?"

"Because you make me feel safe, and you make me feel heard."

I smile, ravished by his unadulterated confession. Stroking and exploring his muscular shoulder absentmindedly with my hand, I admit, "You make me feel safe, too. Emotionally, physically, and mentally."

"That doesn't happen every day, you know."

"No, it doesn't. But that doesn't mean this feels totally comfortable for me, either. I'm not used to being chased by a man. It's an odd experience for me ... very outside of the norm."

"Not used to being chased by guys? I highly doubt that. You're fucking gorgeous. Look at that dumbass employee of yours..."

I shake my head, correcting, "No, I mean being chased by a guy I really want." The words come out unfiltered, thanks to the intensity of our connection and the added persuasion of beer.

Ansel's face lights up with a grin so damn sexy I can't help myself. I lean forward, kissing the dimples in his cheeks. He chuckles, sliding his fingers from mine to capture my head with his hand. Tracing kisses along my collarbone and up my neck, he nibbles and teases the shell of my ear with the tip of his tongue, making me shudder and yearn for more. His fingertips continue circling my hip. Each pass grows bigger and bolder before his lips find mine, claiming me with a mind-numbing, toe-curling kiss.

I can't breathe. I can't think, and I'm pretty damn sure my pulse has stopped. Keep this up, and I'll beg him to take me in the back of his pickup truck. Too bad we sit in a busy lot, even if it is along the wooded edges, affording a little extra privacy.

"You're really good at that." I sigh, reluctantly inching back to breathe, his face still temptingly close to mine.

"I'm good at other things, too."

I giggle. "Like making my brain malfunction and my heart clobber around in my chest."

He grabs my hand, bringing the palm to rest over his heart on his soft, button-down shirt. "You have that effect on me, too."

It thuds against my hand, leaving me bewildered—unable to fully fathom what's going on between us. The moment breeds an out-of-character bashfulness in me, and I train my stare at the blankets we lie on. This man makes me feel everything all at once. I struggle to process so many emotions simultaneously.

"So, how do your relationships usually end?" I ask softly, trying to ground myself and my thoughts.

He cocks his head to the side. "I always end up giving and giving and giving, and my significant other always ends up taking and taking and taking until I'm worn out. About that time, she moves on to a new sucker. How about you?"

I grimace.

"What's wrong?" he asks, his earthy brown eyes washing over my face.

"You stole *my* answer."

"Oh, yeah? I'm sorry. It's a shitty way to conduct relationships."

I nod.

"But it's also got me wondering. What do you think would happen if two givers got together instead of a giver and a taker? You think it might work out?" He eyes me curiously.

"I don't know, and I don't intend to find out because I'm on a work trip. We don't live anywhere near each other, and this just doesn't make sense on any practical level."

"Do you think relationships need to be practical or make sense?"

"Well, yes," I bluster. "If you want them to work."

"What if we quit worrying about the how and focused on the present and what we both want?"

I raise an eyebrow. "And you purport to know what I want?"

He shakes his head with a lopsided grin. "Nope, all I do is keep listening and let you tell me yourself. Your body language speaks volumes."

"You are downright infuriating sometimes."

"Why? Because I call you out? Challenge your assumptions?"

I raise my chin defiantly. "It doesn't really matter since I'll be leaving in a couple of days anyway."

"Then, we better make the most of our time together. Don't you think?"

I open my mouth to speak, but nothing comes out.

"Sorry to change topics, but I will be escorting you back to your room later. You can't say anything to change my mind. I don't trust that guy."

"Okay. And I will hold you to at least one more dance, Stranger. Although I'm curious to see what you have in mind without going back inside Stonie's."

"Okay," he says, lifting his empty beer bottle and shooting a questioning look in my direction. "Another one?"

"Yes, please."

"Alright, then, city girl. Wrap up your grub. You're coming back inside with me."

"You're going to make me go back in there?"

"Yes, I am. It's either that or we walk across the street to the gas station and get a six-pack because I'm not leaving the most beautiful girl I've ever met alone in the dark in the back of my pickup truck."

"Most beautiful?" I snort, certain he has to be joking. No man has ever talked this way about me. But when I look at the mountain man's rugged face, from his straight, well-proportioned nose to his highly kissable lips, sincerity greets me.

His eyes dance over mine for one sensual moment, yearning building in them before he looks away, swallowing hard. "Sometimes I get a little overenthusiastic, as you already figured out. But I never lie."

The corners of my mouth turn up as I nod.

"Anyway," he says, sitting up suddenly and clapping his hands together. "If we're not heading back into Stonie's, let's hit the convenience store at the gas station. I know they have six packs of Rough & Ready Red unless you want to drink something else?"

"No, I prefer local brews, and anything sounds better than dealing with the crowd in there." We both stare at the entrance with its neon sign, hearing the hollow booming coming from the jukebox inside.

Without warning, Ansel jumps down from the raised truck bed, turning and offering me his hands. I bite my bottom lip, instantly self-conscious. "I'm heavier than most girls if you haven't noticed," I say, doing mental gymnastics to figure out how to get down without taking a header, ripping my skirt, or letting him get a sense of my actual weight.

"Let me help you," Ansel says, wrapping his hands around my waist. I can tell he won't take no for an answer. With a sharp exhale, I nod, and he lifts and places me on the ground as if I'm featherlight. The move sets my body on fire, making the juncture at the top of my legs throb. It doesn't get any hotter than that.

He makes me feel things I never get to experience, like being beautiful, dainty, and delicate. But he also instills me with security and peace-of-mind. Like I can finally let down my guard, quit over-functioning, and relax. The sensation is dangerously addictive.

He chuckles, examining my expression closely. "I'm starting to think you're even more antisocial than I am, Annalise."

I frown. "You may be onto something."

"And you're also kind of a grumpy cat, aren't you?"

I chuckle. "More so in the morning."

"This is the second time you've alluded to not liking mornings. So, I take it you're a night owl?"

"More like a swing shifter, if that's a thing. I have the most energy between noon and midnight. But of course, that's not how the world is structured, so I figure it out. Coffee helps."

"How do you take your coffee?"

"French pressed and black," I answer without hesitation.

"Me, too."

"French pressed? Really?"

He nods. "What, you don't think country bumpkins know about things like that?"

I shake my head. "It's not that at all. But I don't know anyone else who does their coffee that way."

He shrugs, grabbing my hand and threading his thick fingers between my smaller ones as we pause, bobbing our heads in both directions before crossing the road to the convenience store. "Well, it's better that way. That's all I know for sure."

"And you take it black, too?" I raise a questioning eyebrow.

"Yep, and only dark roast. I can't handle that light acidic shit they always try to pawn off on people."

"Me either. Maybe we do have more in common than meets the eye."

"Let's wait and see what you're like in the morning," he teases with a shit-eating grin.

"You're incorrigible. You know that, right?"

"When it comes to what I want? Yes, ma'am. Unapologetically so."

One trip to the gas station, a six-pack of beers, and a couple of water bottles later, we dance in the parking lot next to his truck to the tunes pouring from his satellite radio.

My stilettos came off a while ago as Ansel gave me the most delectable foot massage of my entire life. And now, I stand in my stockinged feet atop his big combat boots at the burly mountain man's suggestion. After all, he doesn't want my "pretty feet" to get dirty or hurt.

Ansel has somehow managed to find the most romantic country station possible, and he holds me close, nuzzling my neck and thrilling me with his soft, warm lips and wicked tongue. The throb at the top of my legs is downright painful, and my panties must be dripping. I've never reacted this way to a man in my entire life. It both excites and scares me. I only know one thing. This man is not only accompanying me back to my hotel room. He's staying. End of story.

"You're going to be grumpy as hell for that early morning appointment," he muses, his lips pressed against my décolletage. My heart pounds. All I can think about are his lips descending further—the feel of his hot, velvety tongue on my nipples and far naughtier locations.

"I am," I say, feeling less guilty and more irresponsible than I probably should, thanks to the beer.

"Maybe you could reschedule your plans for a little later?"

His suggestion relaxes my shoulders despite a small inner voice that warns me against the idea. After all, I've pulled off full work days on less sleep than I stand to get tonight if I cut things short with Ansel now. But that's the problem. I don't want to cut anything short with him.

"That's not a bad idea," I say, guilt and pleasure fighting an internal battle.

"It's what I did ... because I'm not ready to say goodnight to you yet."

"And I'm not ready to say goodnight to you," I echo, stealing a glimpse at his gorgeous face. "Although I am ready to go back to my room, if you'd like to join me?"

He raises his thick black eyebrows and clears his throat.

"I mean, to make sure my employee hasn't stolen it or anything..."

"Of course, but I should probably let you know I'm not into casual hookups, one-night stands, and those kinds of things."

My cheeks flush. "What are you into then?" I whisper.

"Spreading the woman I adore out in bed and spending hours worshipping every inch of her body. Learning her with my hands, fingers, and tongue until I know at least seven ways from Sunday how to make her scream."

"Your hands, fingers, and tongue? Aren't you forgetting something?" I ask, my face burning.

"More like saving the best for last."

"Spoken like a man," I grumble, shaking my head.

"Spoken like a man who knows what he's got and how to use it."

"I would need to see that to believe it, Ansel."

"No, you'd need to feel it to believe it. That is, if you trust me?"

"I do." The words escape my lips unthinkingly, but that doesn't make them any less meaningful or sincere. Somehow, out of the crazy chaos of today, Ansel feels like the buoy keeping my head above water.

I hear the click of his truck locks as he reaches into his pocket, pressing the fob, and the radio falls silent. My lower core tightens, my pussy greedy for the man I've spent the evening stoking the fires of sexual tension with. I reach into my pocket, grabbing my phone.

To my relief, I have a text from Ridge Dawson requesting we move our appointment to one in the afternoon. I respond:

Perfect. See you then.

"Why the grin?" Ansel asks.

"Because my plans already got moved to the afternoon. It's perfect."

"It's synchronicity," he says with a satisfied nod.

Even though Dawson, Johnny, and I are all in the same group text, I message the cameraman to be doubly sure he gets the change in plans. More text messages from Mortimer catch my eye, and I work hard to keep my face unreadable.

It won't stop with road rage...

Are you ignoring me?

Answer me or pay the consequences

You're playing with fire, you uppity fucking bitch

A shiver of terror runs the length of my spine, and I swallow hard, trying to remain calm as the blood drains from my face.

"Hey, what's wrong?"

I excuse lamely, "I texted my employee about the meeting time change, but his notifications are silenced. I hope he gets this message in time, and I hope he hasn't tried to steal my room." A part of me longs to tell Ansel about Mortimer Cady and everything going on as a TV producer. But there's so much to explain, and it's honestly not his problem.

"You do realize it's well after midnight? Pretty much the whole world has their notifications off."

"No, there's no—" I clasp my hand over my mouth,

checking the time on my phone, which I overlooked while looking at texts. "How in the hell have we stayed out so late?"

He shrugs. "I guess time flies with you."

"Oh my God. I should go to bed. Seriously."

Ansel shakes his head, pulling me close. "Your plans already got rescheduled, and your employee will figure it out. Besides, you and I both know there will be no sleeping until I take care of a few things for you."

My cheeks must glow like my blouse under the blacklight. "We're both going to be dead to the world tomorrow."

"You don't even know the half of it, Ducky. I never stay up this late," he admits with a large grin, flashing straight, white teeth.

"Ducky? Is that a nickname or something?"

"Sure is."

"And what in the world does it mean?"

"Like a duck swimming on a lake, everything looks calm and placid with you on the surface. But beneath the buttoned-up, professional exterior, your mind is swirling as fast as a duck's legs, going a mile a minute as you try to sort out your worries and thoughts and swim against your present circumstances."

He couldn't be more right. But that doesn't mean I can slow down my thoughts.

My mind travels at lightspeed to reintroduce a little logic to my next decisions, and I introduce another concern. "What about your statement against casual hookups, though?"

The mountain man eyes me warmly. "See what I mean about that noggin of yours? It never stops."

"I don't think so," I confess, wetting my bottom lip with my tongue.

He leans in, murmuring, "I'm going to stop that pretty little head of yours from torturing you. That way, you can get some shuteye."

"And how do you purport to do that?"

"By lighting your body up and filling you with so much pleasure, all you can do is focus on enjoyment."

I whimper, my eyes rounding. I need Ansel so bad I can barely string two thoughts together.

"And for the record, there won't be anything casual about tonight, Annalise."

I should stop this now. But the thought of denying myself the pleasures sure to come is unthinkable. The same goes for the sense of security and comfort I feel in his strong arms. We stop by my car, retrieve my luggage, and then use the other key on the hotel keychain, to let ourselves inside the quaint Victorian mansion turned inn. A handwritten note on the counter reads: "Call (530) 555-0100 if you need help."

"You're not second-guessing yourself?" Ansel asks, sexily furrowing his brow. He knows me too well.

I shake my head, and he grins in a way that makes my heart flutter in my chest and my lower core tighten into a painful ball of need. My nipples are already pebbled and my panties drenched. My body demands every inch of this man. They say men sometimes think with their cock. Well, now I get it, my greedy pussy taking control of the mental reins.

"Good. Because I need you so fucking much," he murmurs darkly, leading me quietly upstairs to the third floor, where the honeymoon suite awaits.

Honeymoon suite? Talk about giving this over-the-top guy the wrong impression! I turn towards him, leaning against the door and warning before we enter, "I kind of failed to mention this before. But this is the honeymoon suite. So, it's kind of overboard in the romance department."

Anger flashes across his face. "See, what I mean about that guy? Only booking one room and the honeymoon suite to boot? That's no accident." He points towards the door. "If he's in there..."

"Shh... We don't want to wake the whole hotel."

Ansel frowns, taking a couple of deep breaths and then forcing his face to relax. "On the other hand... If he isn't in there..." The persistent outdoorsman trails off, boxing me in front of the door and resting his arms on either side of my head. Slowly, he covers the distance between us for the softest, most sensual kiss I've ever experienced. The kind of kiss that makes me free-float from reality, showering my body from head to toe in glimmering, shimmering bliss.

"If he isn't in there... Go on, Romeo..."

Instead of answering, he chuckles in dangerous tones that ratchet the tension in my lower core. *I need Ansel. I need him now.*

Turning to clumsily unlock the hotel room door, I curse under my breath at the clunky key. Where's a swipe card when you need to look smooth?

Chapter Eight

PAIGE

"Romeo? Huh." He gives the room a cursory glance, as do I, finding nothing disturbed by Johnny.

"Yes, because—"

Shutting the door to the room behind us, he pins me against it, capturing my lips with his. His previous kisses have been playful and passionate, but this one is voracious and unhinged. His velvety tongue sweeps into my mouth, unbridling my body from reason and logic and pulling a needy moan from deep within my being as he suggestively penetrates me, making his needs clear with each rhythmic thrust of his tongue.

"Fuck," he whispers, drawing back and resting his lips on the pulse point of my neck, his beard tickling my décolletage. "Do you have any idea how much I need you, Annalise?"

My mouth opens, ready to come clean about my real name. After all, we've moved well past the stranger phase. But his hot lips cover mine again, and his seeking tongue delves into my silky warmth, claiming me and stealing the breath from my lungs.

Lust snakes through my arteries and veins, driving my

76

hands to rove over his body, delighting at every firm, unyielding inch of him. My hands go to his ass, grabbing and savoring his hardness. His hips jut towards my stomach, and the thick outline of his hard rod makes my pussy spasm greedily.

Suddenly, Ansel steps back, seizing me in his arms and carrying me towards the bed. His eyes flicker to the jacuzzi in the massive honeymoon suite, and he says with an incorrigible grin. "Okay, we're definitely fucking in the tub later. But right now, I have to get my first taste of you."

My breath catches in my throat, anticipation drowning my body.

"You like that idea, don't you?" he asks with a pleased grin.

"I do."

He tosses me onto the bed, his eyes branding me with need. My arms stretch out, and I notice the soft feel of rose petals under my fingers. The realization makes me laugh, and it inspires Ansel to eye the room more closely.

"There's champagne chilling on the table," he narrates, nodding towards a metal container with two delicate glass flutes next to it. "And chocolates on the pillows." He holds one up, winking at me. "I've never been on a honeymoon. Is this what it's like?"

"I have no clue," I confess. "I've never been married or even wanted to be."

He opens his mouth to speak, and I expect another one of his cheesy, over-the-top lines. Instead, he presses his lips firmly together, turning his attention to my black stilettos, which he unceremoniously tosses one by one to the ground next to the bed before attacking my tailored a-line skirt, unbuttoning and slipping the slinky fabric over my hips, lamentably revealing control-top pantyhose beneath.

Oh, God. Control-top pantyhose? To claim I wasn't dressing

for sex is the understatement of the year. Does it get more embar-
rassing than this?

Regret fills my head as I wish I was wearing something a
little sexier, like thigh highs with garters. But the burly bearded
man doesn't seem to notice. And if he does, it doesn't hamper
his enthusiasm. In fact, the way he looks at me floods me with
pride. Under his gaze, I'm the most desired woman in the
world ... the only woman in the world. I've never had any man
do this to me before, and it scares and thrills me simultaneously.

My hands go to my blouse, working quickly to
unfasten the little row of buttons that line the front. With
one dramatic flourish, he pulls the pantyhose from my
legs, letting his eyes sink into the shiny satin of my flesh-
colored panties. My cheeks glow as his eyes darken a
couple of shades, noticing the wet spot he's responsible
for.

Propping myself up on my elbows before he can remove
anything else, I shrug out of my coat and then my blouse,
revealing my matching nude bra.

"Are you going to undress, Romeo?" I ask, suddenly
feeling very self-conscious.

"Oh, yeah," he says breathlessly, soaking me in with his
eyes.

"What?" I ask, fighting the urge to shield my body with
my hands.

He runs a hand through his dark hair, looking dumb-
struck. "You're so fucking beautiful. I can't take my eyes off
you."

My cheeks burn. I'm about to remind him this is basically
a one-night stand, and we should keep emotions out of it. But
what we promised earlier rolls back over me ... not to worry
about the future but instead savor the present. And all I can
think about is his head between my thighs.

"I'm clean, and I've got condoms. Although, regrettably, they're back in my truck. Should I go get them?"

I shake my head, alarmed at my unrestrained need for this man. "No, I'm on birth control, and I'm clean, too. Unless you don't feel comfortable going raw?"

He confesses in dark tones, "I don't want any fucking thing between us."

"Neither do I," my wanton mouth replies, overriding the last vestiges of my thinking brain.

"Good," he says, hurrying out of his Carhartt and blue and green flannel shirt. My breath catches in my throat, taking in the stunning gray and black tattoos lining his chest and arms. I read "Carpe Diem," written in script above his carved pectorals and notice the ink peeking around his ribs from back tattoos. My fingers itch to trace the intricate lines, and my body hungers to taste him.

"Turn around," I order breathlessly.

He raises a curious eyebrow, obeying and looking over his shoulder at me.

My eyes follow the lines of his gray and black, hyperrealistic artwork, which include nature scenes, animals, and Marine symbols. I could spend hours tracing and savoring the designs with my fingertips and tongue. I swallow loudly. "Your ink is stunning, Ansel. You're stunning."

"Thank you," he says with a bashful grin. He toes off his boots and shimmies out of his tight-fitting jeans, bringing me a layer closer to his round, muscular ass and thighs. Turning back towards me, he stands in nothing more than a pair of orange-and-gray striped boxer briefs and gray wool socks. Looking down, he chuckles, "Should I take those off?"

"You should take it all off," I encourage greedily.

He chuckles deep in his chest.

Impatience grips me, and my hands start towards the clasp at the front of my bra.

"No, let me do that," he commands. I love the firmness of his tone, like the firmness of his prominent dick in his tented boxer briefs.

He removes his socks quickly before slipping out of his boxers unhesitatingly. My eyes devour his massive rod and the tease of dark hair that pulls my eyes to his large balls. Pleasure dominates my appreciative gaze. "You're a big boy in every way."

"Yes, ma'am."

"Maybe too big for me." I swallow loudly.

He cocks his head to the side, grinning at me and weighing his words. "Part of me wants to tell you we'll figure it out, take things at your pace... But I have a suspicion that's not what you really want to hear."

"And what do you think I want to hear?"

"That you're going to take every fucking inch of me like a good girl."

"Oh," I let out a ragged puff of air. His face is vindicated as he scrutinizes my expression.

"And you're going to like it."

"Yes," I whisper, my heart fluttering.

"But first things first," he says, dropping to his knees in front of me and sliding his hands up the insides of my thighs before demandingly spreading my legs. "I need to get you ready for this long, thick cock."

"Oh?" Desire has devolved my vocabulary down to inarticulate one-syllable questions. "How?"

"By eating you out until you cover my face in your sugar-sweet honey."

I swallow guiltily. Shit, this is the part I never like saying, but I have to do it or waste the whole night on a fruitless venture. Gulping air, I say, "I'm sorry, Ansel, but I won't come."

His eyebrows shoot up into his hairline.

I add, "Like ever. It's never happened before with a man, so there's no need to waste your time on that."

Skepticism etches his face, and a lopsided grin captures his lips. "Ducky, you let me worry about how I waste my time. Okay? Now lie back and relax. Work on being as tranquil mentally as you look physically."

"But—"

"Lie back and relax," he repeats, stroking the insides of my thighs with his fingertips, raising trails of goosebumps and shivers of bliss at every point of contact. "Clear your mind and focus on how my tongue and fingers make you feel. Your clit and your pussy are all that exist now."

"Okay," I reply, wholly unconvinced. The last thing I want is a round of clumsy, semi-painful finger-banging. But something about the look on Ansel's face nudges me to heed his words and stick my legs in the air.

The mountain man's rough, large hands circle my waist, and he squeezes the top of my hips, pulling me demandingly towards the corner of the bed. Then, his hands come up, encouraging me to relax my legs over his shoulders.

Splaying my pussy lips open with his forefinger and thumb, he dives into me, unhesitatingly lapping at my clit before sucking it softly into his mouth. The move drives my fingertips into the mattress, and I let out a whimper, already in uncharted territory with this man. Past boyfriends couldn't even find my clit, but this stranger already owns it.

Moaning against my nub, he fills my lower core with delicious vibrations as he continues swirling and lapping me. "Fuck, you taste so good. Like your flavor was made just for me."

My mind has never been more blank, soaking up the heat of his stimulation. I don't care about anything except the wicked ways his tongue devours me. My hand sinks into his thick, dark hair, holding his ravenous mouth against me.

"Please don't stop, Ansel," I pant, and a growl of desire rips through the man, transporting shivers of desire through me.

His fingers slide through my wet folds, and I stiffen for a moment, not thrilled by the thought of what men in the past have done to try to get me off.

"Relax," Ansel commands, his fingertips teasing my silky folds. I let go of all expectation, sinking into the soft mattress as he gently penetrates me with his finger.

Unlike awkward lovers I've had in the past, he doesn't go for hard and fast. Instead, he explores my pussy gently but firmly, locating the bundle of nerves at the front, which I always target when getting off with my vibrator. A satisfied moan escapes my lips as he strokes me sensually, his finger curling back towards his body as his tongue continues to swirl and twist my nub, sucking it swollen and heightening the heady sensations running the length of my body. He adds a second finger, continuing to pet my G-spot and adding the perfect amount of stretch.

His tongue circles me as my pussy throbs, growing more drenched with each stroke. Naughty, wet noises fill the room as he devours me with his skillful tongue, making my hips buck towards him. No man has ever done this to me; my head spins.

I'm out of control with lust, my drenched channel squeezing and trembling around his slick fingers. My hips strain towards the greedy mouth that continues to undo me with his wicked, hot tongue.

"Ansel." I moan, floating upwards towards the ceiling. Unadulterated ecstasy holds me firmly in its grip as I pant out of my mind with need. "Don't stop. Please."

His tongue swirls and twists me into oblivion, and for the first time in my life, I fall over the precipice of an unnamable, indescribable bliss, coming undone and slamming my hand over my lips to muffle my desperate cries as I scream his name.

My pussy clamps and convulses around him, and he doubles down on licking my clit until I writhe and tremble on the bed.

He chuckles in deep tones, his pleased face perusing mine as he runs a big hand over his beard, sucking the fingers he pleasured me with into his mouth to get every bit of my flavor possible. The move undoes me as I raptly watch.

Suddenly, panic grips me as I struggle to catch my breath. I stare between my legs frantically at him.

"What's that look for?" He growls, crawling up onto the bed and pulling me tightly against his hot core.

"I realize what you just did to me..."

"What? Made you come?"

I nod. "And ruined me for every guy I'll ever be with again and maybe my vibrator, too."

"First off," he says in a dark whisper. "I don't want there to be any other guys after me. It's what I've been doing a terrible job of trying to communicate to you all night. And, second, before we give up on that vibrator, I'd like a chance to use it on you ... along with various other toys."

"What kind of a guy are you?" I ask incredulously. No man has ever talked about pleasuring me like a personal goal.

"The kind of man who wants to make you happy in every fucking way possible. But I know. I know. I continue to move too fast for you. So, suffice it to say, there are no lengths I won't go to in order to make you back-clawing, name-screaming, pussy-trembling satisfied."

"Pussy-trembling? You really don't have a poetic bone in your body."

He laughs. "Not especially. But I've got another bone, and I swear you'll like it far better anyway. Ready to see if we can make it fit?"

"Fuck, yes," I exclaim, still out of my mind with want. There's pretty much nothing this man could suggest that I would say "no" to in my current state. "How do you want to do this?" I pant.

"I want you to ride this thick cock."

"Yes." Electricity lights up the air as he repositions, lying on the bed with the pillows under his head. With a big grin and an impatient hand gesture, he bids me to climb on top of him.

I straddle him with my knees bent on either side of his hips. His eyes simmer as I spit on my hand, dropping it between my legs to stroke the length of his massive, hard rod. He lets out a pleasurable groan as my hand slides up and down, marveling at his size and firmness.

"Are you ready for this?" I tease, hovering over him and sliding his large tip through my drenched folds.

"Yes, Annalise. There's nothing I want more."

"Good," I say, sliding slowly down over his rod and sheathing him in my silky warmth, savoring every inch. He shudders, a deep, resonant growl rumbling from his chest as I work my thighs back and forth, taking him more deeply with each pass. His eyes roll back in his head, and his hips inch toward mine as I ride him into ecstasy.

Ansel's girth pushes my pussy to the edge of pleasure and pain, filling me with a sensation I never want to let go of. I had no idea how empty and lonely I was until this moment with this man filling and completing me.

Sitting up, he unclasps the front of my bra, devouring my tits with his eyes. Leaning back on his elbows, he chases my breasts, capturing my right nipple in his mouth and sucking it with glee. My heart pounds as I continue to slip up and down his rod, eliciting more deep-throated growls and groans. I match his sensual utterances with my own breathy, high-pitched whimpers, sighs, and moans.

His big tongue swirls my areola with increasing intensity, alternating teasing nibbles and twists of his tongue that make my breath catch in my throat. Hungrily sucking and working me into a frenzy, he doesn't stop until they form two hard peaks. He spreads his legs, bending his knees to trap the backs of my ankles with his calves, leveraging deeper into my pussy.

I gasp, increasing the speed and depth of my downward thrusts, falling in love with his rod.

His pelvis is tireless, arching up into me. His hands possessively seize my hips, changing the angle until he finds the sweet spot, crashing again and again into the bundle of nerves at the front of my pussy.

My channel grows slicker and tighter, squeezing painfully towards a second climax. *Two in one night from the same man? No vibrator needed?* I had no clue this was possible.

Ansel pulls me demandingly into him, going deeper with each pass until he's seated to the hilt inside me. I moan, closing my eyes and leaning forward so that my breasts rub over his soft, furry chest, lighting up my nipples. The angle brings the full focus of his cock to my G-spot as I close my eyes, panting and moaning. His mouth crashes into mine, claiming me hungrily.

"Goddamn, Ducky, your pussy was made for me."

I can't help but giggle between pants. His nickname for me isn't especially sexy but as quirky as he is.

He opens one mahogany eye, arching his brow—a question on his face.

"Just your nickname for me. That's all," I explain, letting him know why I'm laughing.

Closing his eyes again, he strains toward self-control, and he asks breathily, "Is it any weirder than the fact we're using each other's middle names?"

I shake my head. But there's something undeniably sexy and forbidden about the anonymity.

"The way your pussy grips me is fucking addictive. I may

85

have to keep you," he says, opening both eyes to gauge my reaction.

I have no clue why, but my treacherous mouth smiles broadly, and my cheeks punctuate the inexplicable response with a radiant glow. Instead of protesting his plans, I reach back behind me, grabbing and gently stroking his balls.

"Fuck!" he pants, his face betraying how he comes a little more undone with each stroke. I love having this kind of power over such a monstrously big guy while acknowledging how thoroughly the pleasures of his skilled tongue, mouth, and fingers have vanquished me.

"Your pussy's silky perfection." He groans, fighting a losing battle with restraint as I continue to ride his throbbing dick, his pelvis rising to meet mine greedily.

He spits on his thumb, bringing it between our bodies to rub my clit. As his rough, slick thumb masters my nub again, I feel myself in free fall. My lower abdomen tightens along with my pussy, and I come hard, drenching his cock and balls as my muscles jump and my channel clenches and releases rhythmically to the tapping of his thumb on my swollen clit.

The mountain man screams, following me over the same cliff of sheer pleasure. His hips jut up into me as thick, hot waves of cum flood me. His massive hands squeeze my hips urgently, mixing pleasure with pain.

I'm almost certain I'll have bruises tomorrow. But even more than that, I'll be ruined for any guy that follows Ansel. Maybe, as the mountain man has suggested, I should find a way to keep him.

He pulls me into his arms, showering my face in featherlight kisses as he encourages me to settle on his warm, furry chest. "It's official," he teases, a tinge of urgency in his voice. "I won't let you leave me, Annalise, or whatever you really call yourself."

His eyes search mine questioningly. No man has ever looked at me like this after sex.

Heck, who am I kidding? They're usually too busy finding their clothes, dressing, and leaving. I haven't slept with many men, thanks to the disappointing nature of the encounters. But I realize in shock that Ansel isn't about to leave me, and he needs more.

Stroking my hair tenderly, he says, "That wasn't a one-and-done, right? You felt what I felt?"

My fingers trace the angular line of his inked pecs as I softly kiss his chest. Even stranger than his question about what I felt is my answer. "Yes, I felt what you felt." How can I make such a claim? Am I suddenly a mind reader? But despite an answer completely untethered from reality, I know deep in my core I'm stating the truth.

"Good," he says, leaning forward to kiss the top of my head. "You've been worth the wait. Every fucking, excruciating minute of it."

Again, his words make no sense in the context of our meeting this afternoon. But I have the strange impression his soul is speaking to mine as I answer, "So have you."

Chapter Nine

RIDGE

"**S**hit!" Annalise's voice forces my eyes open. Memories from last night rush over me, filling my core with heat. My delirious eyes pop open, straining to understand her exclamation.

"What's wrong?" I grumble.

"I'm going to be late. Dammit! I have to get ready, and you have to go."

"What time is it?"

"Eleven fifty." Her voice trembles.

"Fuck!" I sit up, scrubbing my face with my palms. Isolated images from last night fill my mind.

The way she moaned and held my head locked against her as I buried my tongue in her sweet pussy. How she rode me on the bed, her tits bouncing and begging me to claim them with my mouth. The steamy jacuzzi session afterward, where we cleaned up and teased each other before a mind-blowing session of sixty-nine. And then, early this morning, when morning wood pulled me from my dreams, she snuggled invitingly against me, raising her ass at the perfect angle to suck me into her slick pussy while my hands teased and played with her ample tits.

Never have I experienced a more affectionate or generous lover. My thoughts grow dark and possessive. I can't go back now. I have to find a way to make this woman mine forever.

But dammit! I absolutely have to get to my appointment. Now, more than ever, I need a thriving career with the funds to support Annalise. There's so much convincing I have yet to do when it comes to our current situation. I need money and success to show her I'm more than a good fuck.

Doing the mental math to get to my place, I realize I have to go now. My heart aches at the thought, wondering if I'll ever see her again. But I have to have faith in the feelings flowing between us. Otherwise, why would fate lead me to this beauty in the first place? Jumping out of bed, I slip begrudgingly into my clothes, each garment putting a barrier back between me and Annalise.

She follows behind me, racing around the room frantically. "I need a quick shower and... Oh, I can't believe how irresponsible I've been." Her voice is grumpy, and her face looks pissed as hell.

Even as we speak, I'm running out of time, but I still offer. "I'll grab us some coffee at Sweet Rush. I'll be right back."

"Thank you," she says, palming my cheeks and reaching up on her tiptoes to kiss my lips.

As I race down the stairs of the bed and breakfast, Mrs. Chatterton's eyes round. I've never stayed here before, although I know the old lady well. She gave me my first job mowing lawns. My cheeks burn as she asks, "Why, Ridge, what are you doing here?"

"Helping out a friend." I feel like a kid in the principal's office, saying the first thing that comes to mind.

"Oh," she says, raising her eyebrows and eyeing my untucked flannel shirt.

It hits me all at once: bed *and* breakfast. Duh! What am I thinking? "Mrs. Chatterton, do you have any strong, black coffee brewed?"

"Well, of course, sweetie. Breakfast is in the salon," she invites with a smile. Almost as an afterthought, she adds in a scolding whisper, "But it's for guests."

"Fortunately, my friend is a guest. May I help myself to some for ... them?"

"Yes," she says, her eyes still large as she tries to process everything.

In the Victorian salon, I find a couple of tables set up with chairs and a beautiful spread. The food looks like it's been picked over, and I note the sign on the side table warning that breakfast ends at noon. Just squeaking in by the skin of my teeth. I grab two disposable cups, filling them to the top with black coffee before adding lids and racing past Mrs. Chatterton in the lobby. With a polite nod, I round the stairs to the third floor.

I knock softly on the door, and Annalise lets me in, her hair damp from the shower. Her citrus vanilla smell wraps around me. "Damn, you're beautiful," I exclaim, savoring a kiss before handing her a cup of coffee. "I can't vouch for how good this is, but that's what they had downstairs. I owe you a good French press later."

"Thank you," she grumbles, her lips pressed firmly together. Damn, she *is* grumpy in the morning. Wrapping her hands around the cup and blowing on the steaming liquid, she takes a few sips, closing her eyes. Finally, her expression relaxes, and her eyelids flutter open. "Coffee makes everything better."

I level my gaze on her, loath to leave. But I have to. Leaning in to kiss her, I excuse, "Sorry to drink coffee and run, but I can't miss this appointment."

"Okay," she freezes, staring expectantly at me.

"But I'll be back tonight, so don't even think about leaving me yet."

Her face softens. "Good, because I have to see you again."

"I have to see you, too." I wink. Talk about the understatement of the year! "Have a great work meeting, and I'm all yours tonight, Ducky. Be sure to let me in when I knock."

"Alright, Romeo. Why don't you try working on a sexier nickname before you come back tonight?"

"Sexier?" I pause in thought. "How about sweet lips?"

She giggles, "Keep trying. Bye, handsome."

"Later," I promise, kissing her one last time. I race downstairs, bidding Mrs. Chatterton goodbye before sprinting across the street to my truck. The blankets and to-go boxes remain piled in the bed, filling my brain with delicious memories of last night and the woman of my dreams.

Sitting in my truck, I open my phone, shooting the TV people I'm slated to meet a quick text, excusing myself and instructing them to give Sweet Rush a try before heading my way. The bakery is owned by my sister-in-law, Cricket, and I've never steered anyone wrong with its delectable pastries, sandwiches, and treats.

I notice a confirmation text sent last night for the time change, kicking myself for not checking this sooner. What has Annalise done to my mind? I haven't been this irresponsible since before my Marine days.

Even now, scolding myself, the thought of the pretty woman with long raven-colored hair does crazy things to my body. My pulse pounds and my blood heats in my veins. I have to see her again. And even more than that, I have to find a way to make her mine and keep her that way.

Chapter Ten

PAIGE

I n the bed and breakfast parking lot, Johnny loiters, his face embittered. He makes an obvious point of staring at his watch, scolding, "We're late."

"I know," I grumble, clinging to the coffee cup Ansel gave me like it's a lifeline. To say I'm grumpy in the morning is an understatement, especially *this* morning. Not so much because of the delicious pleasures of last night or even the countless beers I downed, but because now I have to wake up and try to function as a professional again. How do you do that after a night spent behind paradise's gates?

Ansel's words echo in my head. *"I'll be back tonight, so don't even think about leaving me yet."* My pulse races at the thought. I have to see the mountain man again, no matter how illogical or impractical it seems.

I wear a pair of tailored, no-iron (thankfully!), wide-leg navy blue slacks with beige leather loafers and a navy and white striped, three-quarter-length sleeve knit top. Accents include simple gold stud earrings and a gold charm bracelet commemorating the places my work has taken me over the years.

My hair is air-dried and wavy with a little oil rubbed in to help the shine. Although I would normally blow it out and curl the ends, it has a surprisingly cute, relaxed beach vibe, and I've got sparse makeup on for a natural, pretty look. Polished on the surface, I feel full of turmoil beneath it—a great heaping swirl of stress, elation, worry, ecstasy, and self-chastising. Just like Ansel's "Ducky" nickname suggests.

I can't help but laugh to myself, thinking back on last night as I climb into my sleek, sporty Fiat, musing at its diminutive size next to Johnny's big white, windowless "kidnapper" van. And he wanted me to sleep in my car. Ridiculous!

"I've dropped a pin to his cabin, but you can follow me as I've mapped out the whole thing. Not sure your Black Widow will make it all the way, though." Johnny murmurs.

"What do you mean?"

"There's a good chunk of the road that's unpaved."

"Yikes!"

He shrugs. "Just follow me, and if it seems like it's getting too hairy for you, honk, and I may consider giving you a ride the rest of the way."

"Whatever." I shake my head. It's a good thing he's such a fantastic wilderness cameraman because his morose, butthurt personality leaves a lot to be desired.

Setting my navy blue Coach handbag on the passenger seat, I pull out my phone to find Johnny's pin and start my maps app. I see a new text from Ridge Dawson.

> I'm running a few minutes late. Sorry

> Maybe kill some time by grabbing coffee at Sweet Rush?

> Already have coffee in hand but running a little late, too, so this works. See you soon

I let my shoulders relax slightly, stepping back out of the car to relay the gist of it to Johnny. He lets out an angry groan as he stretches, taking pains to make sure I notice. "If I'd known we would have so much extra time to kill this morning, I would have stayed in Ophir City, after all."

"You should have," I say flatly, not about to get suckered into feeling sorry for him.

"And you should have gone to bed at a decent time."

I shake my head, enraged by his statement, even though I know he's entirely right. "Were you spying on me?" I narrow my eyes.

"Didn't have to. You woke me out of a sound sleep, laughing and whispering your way into the bed and breakfast." He looks disgusted.

I don't give a fuck.

"Have you watched any of Dawson's videos yet? Or looked at Steph's sizzle reel?"

His words find their mark, and I examine the pavement, guilt twisting my stomach.

"I guess you have your own way of negotiating, though," he says darkly.

Own way of negotiating? What in the hell is he alluding to? I don't acknowledge his out of line words with a reply. Instead, I give myself an internal pep talk. "You've got this, Paige. You'll have Dawson in contract before you know it. And then..." My thoughts fly to Ansel, my heart pounding behind my ribs.

And then what? You'll try to make a doomed long-distance relationship work? My stomach roils, but I remind myself this time is different. Ansel isn't like other men.

Fate put him in my path for a reason, so I need to have a little faith in The Universe that, somehow, this will all work out. I think of the manifestation audiobooks I listen to. After knowing what I want and asking for it, faith is key. Yet faith has always eluded me. Likely because I had very little I could trust as a child. This time is different, though. I have to believe this.

"So, we're heading to Sweet Rush to grab breakfast before meeting with Dawson? Why doesn't he just meet us there?" the cameraman asks, his eyes straining towards Stonie's across the street.

I scold, "We've already rescheduled this meeting twice. I'm not going to put this man out any more than we have to."

"Whatever," he mutters, holding his hands up, palms facing me. "You're the expert in contract negotiation. I'm just here for the fucking ride."

After walking to Sweet Rush and getting a French press of coffee that's as good as Ansel promised with a flaky, buttery croissant, Johnny and I head back to our vehicles, ready to start our trek into Rough & Ready Country.

Forty painstaking minutes later, we follow a long, smooth gravel driveway, stopping at a stunning two-story, A-frame cabin with floor-to-ceiling windows that must offer pristine views of the lush, verdant wilderness enveloping us.

I park next to Johnny's truck, assuming Dawson's vehicles must be in his garage. Still, my stomach churns, and I hope he's home and not stringing us along. Phil and Steph's warnings fill my head as I stride toward the massive wooden front door, pressing the white doorbell next to it. I hear shuffling and noises behind the door, and a male voice hollers, "Be right there!"

My first thought is: *Dawson's as disorganized as I am today.* My second thought warms my cheeks. *That voice sounds awfully familiar.*

The door opens, and a hulk of a man peers down at me, his hair and beard damp and soft from a shower, the smell of foresty soap filling me with instant recognition. "Ansel!" I exclaim, narrowing my eyes and scrutinizing his face. "What are you doing here?"

"I could ask you the same, Annalise," he replies, a sudden foreboding in his voice.

Johnny barks impatiently behind us. "What the fuck is wrong with you two? After last night, I hardly think I need to make introductions. Paige, this is Ridge Dawson. Dawson, meet my 'boss' Paige Laurier."

My jaw hits the welcome mat, and Ansel laughs deep in his throat. The kind of laugh that says Johnny is out of his freaking mind. But then he stops, scrutinizing my face and clearing his throat.

My head spins. I have just officially fucked up my career in ways I can't even begin to quantify. Phil's words of warning wash back over me. *Just be sure not to fall in love with a cowboy or mountain man while you're there." What in the hell have I done?*

Anger seizes me, looking for a place to land. I turn towards Johnny, questioning, "You knew this was Dawson? Why didn't you tell me?"

"Of course I did, Paige, because I did my fucking research. And I tried to tell you at the bar, but you clearly weren't interested in listening."

"Tried to tell me. How?" I challenge.

"Remember when you said you wanted to get a *feel* for Military Mountain Man's town, and I gestured towards Dawson and corrected, *you mean get a feel for him*?"

"There's a lot of ways you could interpret that statement, Johnny."

He shrugs. "Not my problem."

"Paige?" Ridge repeats, staring at me with rounded eyes.

"Yes," I say, shaking my head. Turning on my heels, I storm away towards the tree line, calling over my shoulder, "I need a moment, please."

Johnny laughs bitterly. "Mind if I shoot a little B-roll footage with Dawson?"

I'm too overwhelmed by everything to breathe, let alone think and offer a fully formed answer to his question. Instead, I pace back and forth at the edge of the woods, my mind racing. *What in the hell have I done? And how can I begin to fix this?*

"B-roll?" I hear Johnny repeat.

"Whatever, man. Film away in my cabin and backyard. But give me a moment with Ann—I mean, Paige, okay?"

Johnny's caustic laugh travels to the edge of the forest, where I continue pacing back and forth. I hear footfalls headed my way and can't look up even when Ridge's deep voice grumbles, "Did you have any idea about this last night?"

His innocent question makes me want to explode. "I don't know, Mr. Dawson. Does it look like I had any idea? Oh my God! What have I done?" I return to pacing, willing the world to stop and give me a few moments to catch up.

"Mr. Dawson?" he repeats uneasily.

"Did *you* have any idea?" I ask, my voice rising with anger.

"Hell, no. Although it doesn't really change anything on my end."

"Well, it changes everything on mine!" I hiss, burying my head in my hands.

"Does it? Really?" He steps towards me, his voice soft and tender. But I can't do this with him. I can't believe what I've done. I shake my head backing up. Concern floods his face.

"Yes." I sigh sharply, eyeing the muscular mountain man. He takes the hint, leaning against a large evergreen with his arms crossed and his countenance somber. "I *never* mix business with pleasure."

"And you still haven't, Paige. God, it's going to take me a while to get used to your name." The big man shakes his head.

"And how haven't I?"

"Because I haven't signed any paperwork yet."

His words put a hollow hope in my heart. Technically, he's correct. But that also means I have a vested interest in working *against* my intended goal—not having him sign the contract—so that I can see him again without trampling on my personal ethics. This sucks! And who am I kidding? Once Johnny tattles back to Phil about me... Just the thought of my mentor's disappointed face makes me nauseous.

"Hey," Ridge comforts me. "We'll get through this together, Ducky. Just take a deep breath and look at me."

My eyes flutter up to his, and my heart stops again. For like the millionth time since I've met this gorgeous man. I inhale slowly, trying to ground myself, but the emotions washing over me are so powerful that I feel like a drowning person in the ocean, untethered and battered by the tide.

He steps forward, conviction in his gaze as he takes my hands, and I look guiltily towards the spot where Johnny last stood. But the cameraman has disappeared, to my relief.

"He's out back filming. Calm down, Paige. We're going to get through this together, and we're going to figure out how to make this work. On the bright side, you've got me right where you want me in these contract negotiations. On the downside, you'll suffer if I settle for less than the best in this deal."

"Why will I suffer?" My voice shakes.

"Because I already told you. I don't do one-night stands or casual hookups. One way or the other, I'm keeping you. So the sweeter the deal I get, the better it will be for both of us."

"You don't get it," I say, slipping my hands from his and returning to marching to and fro. "I've fucked up everything about this deal. And now, thanks to Johnny, my executive producer will find out. I could kick myself for being so unpro-fessional."

"Ducky, take a deep fucking breath and relax."

My eyes lock with his, catching a hint of ambivalence.

"I do have one question, though..."

"What?" I ask, cocking my head to the side.

"How did you not recognize me last night? I mean, you were sent here to get me to sign a contract. Didn't you watch some of my videos and the sizzle Steph submitted?"

Great, now I have to admit I'm incompetent on top of it. "Steph's out for ankle surgery."

He nods. "Yeah, she texted me when the group chat switched, and you were added."

I nod. "I was called in as her last-minute replacement two days ago. Last night was supposed to be when I binge-watched your channel, getting caught up on who you are and what you do. Instead, I was busy with other things."

He chuckles, nodding. "That would be my fault. Although I must say, you know me far better than any YouTube video could have done."

"First of all, it's my fault for not having even a modicum of self-control. Second, what I know about you has nothing to do with this assignment. It's neither appropriate nor professional."

"Hey, Paige. What did I tell you when we first met? Some rules are made to be broken."

I bite my lower lip, looking away.

The large man closes the distance between us, snagging my chin with his finger and forcing me to look at him. "We can get through this... Hell, we can get through anything together. But I am in a quandary."

"A quandary?" I ask, looking up into his stunning earth-colored eyes.

"Why?"

"Because now I'm inclined to say yes to all your demands as a production company representative. But at the same time, I need the best deal possible to be the man you need, and so I can take care of you better."

99

"See? This situation is impossible."

"No offense, Paige. But you need to revamp your definition of 'impossible.' Distinguishing the bad from the good guys during overwatch? Sometimes, that felt pretty fucking impossible. But I never fucked it up. I need you to trust me not to fuck it up now because whether you want to hear this or not, you're the best thing that's ever happened to me. And I can't stand the thought of us not working out."

I try to look down at the forest floor, but he won't let me. Tilting my chin up, he repeats, "You're the best thing that's ever happened to me." He smiles tenderly, leaning down to lightly kiss me.

My eyes wander towards the cabin, where Johnny might be, but thankfully, I don't see him. "So, what do we do now?" I ask breathlessly.

"Help me negotiate the most mutually beneficial contract for your company and our future."

I shake my head, trying to shrug away from him, but he won't let me. "You don't get it. I have conflicting interests now. Somebody else needs to do this."

He crosses his arms, frowning. "How about I tell you exactly what I wanted from In the Haystack before you walked into my life? Then, you tell me what In the Haystack is proposing, and we go from there?"

"You make it sound so simple..."

"None of this is simple. It's complicated as hell. But it's not impossible. Trust me. Now, let's see how good those negotiating skills of yours are."

I nod, feeling both resigned and relieved. "Before we go any further, I need to call my boss and give him a full disclosure of what's happened."

"If that's what you need to do, I'll show you to the guest room, where you're guaranteed quiet and privacy. And then,

I'll get to work on that French press of coffee I promised you. Sound good?"

"Yes, Ans—I mean, Ridge."

A rich, resonant laugh rumbles from his chest. "That may be the hardest part about this whole situation, learning to use each other's real names."

I grin despite myself, still blown away by the situation but starting to find some humor in its irony.

The call with Phil goes far better than planned, although I realize I'll never live it down. The initial surprise is greatly softened by Meredith, who not only intervenes on my behalf but gets on the phone to give me a pep talk about love and how unexpected it can sometimes be. It's a romantic version of carpe diem.

I don't know how I feel about using the four-letter word that starts with "L" in Ridge's context. But my heart soars every time I think about him. And I can't deny the emotions heaped high between us—warm affection, passionate need, and genuine loyalty.

Phil takes over contract negotiations himself, with me listening and interjecting as needed as he and Ridge hash out everything over the phone. "We better get this done before you become my son-in-law," he teases as the two go back and forth. I'm impressed by Ridge's astute negotiating skills, adding yet another pro to my growing list of reasons the mountain man is a dreamboat.

After contracts are signed and we hang up with Phil, Johnny leaves unceremoniously, with plenty of B-roll filmed to start padding scenes. Ridge pulls me enthusiastically into his arms, kissing the top of my head as I rest my cheek against his firm, angular chest. "See? Everything's falling into place. You have nothing to worry about."

"I'm going to hold off judgment until I get back to SoCal and see how Phil treats me moving forward."

"About that. Do you really need to leave me?"

"I do," I whisper softly, kissing his chest.

He runs his large hand through my hair, letting his fingers sensually massage my scalp. "I assume you're based in LA, then?"

I grimace, reminding him, "It's more than a seven-hour drive."

He waves off my concern. "It's less than a two-hour flight from Sacramento. Time to start racking up my frequent flier miles."

I sigh. "Maybe. Or we could recognize this for what it is. A beautiful moment in time. But one we can't hold onto." The words sound hollow, and my chest aches. But I have to say them, give Ridge the option that still makes the most sense to me.

"We live in the same damn state, and we're going to make this work. Now, why don't you let me give you the informal tour of my cabin before rocking your wildest fucking dreams?"

"Mm..." I moan, letting my mind wander. "Kind of like you did last night?"

"Kind of, but I've got plenty of new tricks up my sleeve, too."

"Like what?" I ask breathlessly.

"Like bending you over the back of my couch and eating you out from behind. Then, wrapping your thick locks around my hand and whispering dirty promises into your ear while I fuck you mindless from behind, making you beg for every inch of this thick, juicy cock."

Shivers of desire travel up and down my spine, coalescing at the top of my legs. I need him so much I can barely think. Until sudden apprehension seizes me. "But none of this changes the fact I am now breaking one of my cardinal rules, mixing business with pleasure."

"I can think of worse things. It works for some couples."

"Like Sonny and Cher," I say grumpily.

"How about Blake Shelton and Gwen Stefani?"

"Justin Timberlake and Brittany Spears," I counter.

"Johnny Cash and June Carter."

"You are still incorrigible, even with a new name and identity."

"Yes, ma'am. Time to get used to it."

"There's a lot I have to get used to and plenty I need to think about..."

"Don't think too hard, Ducky."

I shrug, staring at his stunning face and losing myself in his eyes. "I've got some phone calls to make and my bags to pack. And by all rights, I should surrender my key to Mrs. Chatterton so the maids can clean up, and Johnny can stay there tonight."

"And where are you staying?" the gruff mountain man asks in raw tones, stepping closer and wrapping me in his muscular arms.

"Here, if you'll have me?"

He breaks into an ear-to-ear grin. "Hell, yeah, I'll have you. Just don't be surprised when I refuse to let you leave."

"I can think of worse things," I whisper, a seductive throb in my voice. It matches the tight pulse between my legs, but I can't give in to temptation yet.

"Can I help you with anything?"

I shake my head. "I have to get my affairs in order. Call Steph, so she doesn't have to hear about this secondhand, and try to wrap my head around everything that's happened. I just need a little time. I'll call you when I'm headed back your way."

The corners of his mouth turn down. "Okay, but don't stay away for too long, Paige. I want to hear you scream my real name the next time I make you come."

Chapter Eleven

PAIGE

D espite Ridge's comforting words and Phil's ambivalent response to admitting I've done expressly what he forbade, the gears in my head rumble and whirl as I drive back to Hollister and the bed and breakfast. So much has happened in less than twenty-four hours that I can't fathom.

I'll need months of reflection before I can sort out my emotions and come to terms with everything. But my feelings for Ridge make taking that time improbable because, with each passing moment around the man, I fall further down the slippery slope that began last night with a twirl on the dance floor.

I need his strength and comfort. I need his reassurance and how he makes me feel like the most precious thing on this Earth. I need to go deeper with him and explore what it means to be in a relationship with a fellow giver rather than a taker. From what I've seen so far, it's an experience like none other. Cathartic, soul-stirring, edifying.

Back at the bed and breakfast, I inform Mrs. Chatterton about the change of plans, offering her an extra tip for cleaning and tidying up the room. Then, I head upstairs, texting Johnny before hurriedly packing, my mind flooded with thoughts of my handsome mountain man.

Ridge Ansel Dawson. How long will it take me to get used to his real name? I don't know. But I see him everywhere in the hotel room we shared last night, from the rose petals on the bed to the disheveled covers, the half-finished bottle of champagne, empty chocolate wrappers, and the damp towels we used to dry off after the jacuzzi.

My cheeks burn, replaying so many sensual pleasures and realizing there's nothing wrong with me after all. I can orgasm and enjoy sex in wildly satisfying, unhinged ways ... with the right man.

The right man. Those three words make my heart skitter. At thirty-two, I had started wondering if I would ever find the so-called right guy. But I didn't even know what those words truly meant until yesterday, after meeting Ridge.

Worry and thoughts of resignation give way to excitement and hope for the future. Instead of viewing the last day as a career clusterfuck, I start to reshape the narrative.

Maybe The Universe is nudging me towards a better work-life balance. Perhaps it's telling me that love is just as important as ambition, even more so, and that I need to take risks every now and again and break a few rules to claim the future intended for me. A future so much brighter, more colorful, and more intense than I ever could have imagined for myself.

As I finish packing and head downstairs with my luggage, leaving the room key with Mrs. Chatterton and wishing her farewell, I have to stop and pinch myself. I feel like I'm walking in a dream. My thoughts keep tugging incessantly towards the hunky, black-bearded mountain man who spoiled the hell out of me last night. I can't wait to see him again. I need to do it as soon as possible. Every cell in my body testifies to this soul-deep craving.

On the way to Ridge's cabin, I put Steph on the hands-free device, filling her in on everything. She sounds as giddy as a schoolgirl as she squeals into the phone.

"Oh, my freaking gosh! Are you serious? Ridge Dawson? What a hunk!" she whispers the last sentiment, which lets me know Tom must be in hearing range.

I add, "And beyond looks, he's absolutely amazing. So sweet and kind. He listens to me with this intensity that makes me feel truly heard in ways I've never experienced before. You know what I mean?"

"I do. It's the same with lover boy," she agrees, chuckling. She must cover the speaker with her phone because her voice suddenly becomes too muffled to hear, and my ears register deeper tones in the background. Returning to the line, she squees, forcing me to turn the volume down slightly. "I am so freaking unbelievably happy for you! And all I had to do was break my ankle to make this happen."

"It sounds terrible when you put it that way." I glance at my dashboard, suddenly noticing two new red warnings—the coolant and check engine lights. *What in the world?*

"Paige, are you still there?" Steph's words make me realize I've tuned out of our conversation.

My chest tightens, and my pulse races. "Yeah, hold on a sec..." I scan the twisting, two-lane road for a place to pull over. Thankfully, I've had no one behind me on this trip. But when my eyes flicker to the rearview mirror, I realize that's changed. *Dammit!* "Hey, Steph, can I give you a call right back? I've got my hands kind of full at the moment."

"Yeah, sure, I can't wait to hear more about your hunky man."

I laugh weakly, clicking the end call button. A broad embankment welcomes me up ahead as I watch my engine temperature gauge climb. The engine stalls out mid-roll, and I have just enough momentum to pull onto the embankment and watch the gauge plunge back down.

The white dually behind me follows, and bile rises in my throat. I gulp air, bite my bottom lip, and try to take a deep breath. Two men jump out of the truck behind me wearing black and white suits. The driver has strawberry blond hair and beard, a long face, and that short nose I can never forget.

"God help me!" I exhale. My heart races as they draw nearer, wearing the telltale uniforms of the House of the Seven Prophets. I lock my doors, fumbling for my phone in my navy blue Coach purse next to me. When I find it, I drop a pin for Ridge along with the only message I can get off before they start knocking loudly on my driver and passenger windows:

ID2GAT123

The men are tall, their heads well above my windows. They must lean down and peer in to see me. I take advantage of this, tossing my phone under the passenger seat. I hope that law enforcement can use it to locate where things headed south. I also hope it'll quickly alert authorities to the fact I've been taken against my will. The knocking on the windows grows louder, and the blond man finally crouches down, screaming, "Roll down the window!" I hesitate, and he raises his hand until I stare down the barrel of his handgun.

Unblinking, I can't process what's happening. It feels like a nightmare ... one I can't wake up from as I comply, lowering it a sliver.

"Time to start cooperating, Ms. Laurier, or I can guarantee you won't like what comes next." The words put a shiver down my spine, not only because of the speaker's calculated delivery but also because he quotes something I said to Mortimer Cady during our last interview for the TV series.

I clear my throat, attempting to stay calm. "Brandishing a weapon to intimidate someone is illegal."

He chuckles. Suddenly, his face transforms back into menacing, hard stone. "Ms. Laurier, brandishing firearms is the least of your worries now. Step out of the vehicle, and keep your hands where I can see them. Or your life's story will end along with your investigative passions."

I tremble, and the backs of my eyes sting. But I work hard to master myself, taking deep breaths and struggling to remain stable and strong as I step out of the car with my palms facing the man. Internally, I pray for help. Assistance of some kind. All I need is one car to drive by. One person to witness what's going on in broad daylight and then alert the appropriate authorities.

"Face the vehicle and place your hands on the doorframe."

My breath comes faster now as I comply, vulnerability coursing through my veins. The second man, also bearded with chestnut-colored hair, presses firmly against me from behind as my stomach knots. He grabs one wrist at a time, twisting my arms behind my back and handcuffing me. They have handcuffs?

I scold myself internally for still being surprised by this crew. After all, from their lowest rung of farmers and truckers to the upper echelons of law enforcement, judges, legislators, local politicians, congresspeople, and senators, the House of the Seven Prophets have infiltrated the system, using the loyalty of their clandestine, religious-infused mafia to facilitate human trafficking, pedophilia, child marriage, and polygamy. They likely also have ties to the drug trade and cartels south of the border, where some of their outermost communities are located.

The man ties a bandana around my mouth to silence me before throwing a feed sack over my head to blind me. He throws me sideways in the back of the truck's extended cab before the brunette ties my feet, binding the rope to my hand-cuffs to hog-tie me.

I can't sit up. I can't move. I can't see what's going on, and I no longer have my phone. But it remains a distant hope strewn beneath the passenger seat of my car along with the pin and message I managed to get off to Ridge. But my stomach twists and roils as I realize I haven't shared anything about the House of the Seven Prophets with him yet. I was going to confide in him about it tonight when things settle down a bit. The last few days have been insane.

All I can hope is he secures my phone, finds a way to access its data, and gets in touch with Phil, who knows more about this case than anyone. Hot tears pour down my cheeks as open denial of what's going on slowly crumbles into palpable fear.

My body trembles, and I struggle to take deep breaths through my nose. My mind reverts to Ridge and the way he calmed and comforted me when I was stressed out. I relax the muscles in my body, one group at a time, mindfully inhaling and exhaling through my nose as mental clarity slowly returns.

I have an advantage. A distinct one so many of this cult's other victims have never had. I know the organization better than most, and I'm especially familiar with Mortimer Cady, having interviewed him on several occasions for my documentary series, *Growing Up Penitent*.

I portrayed the show to Cady as a fluffy version of *Growing Up Amish*, only among the House of the Seven Prophets, to earn his trust. I'd bet money I'm on my way to speak with him now. The question is, how do I use my knowledge of the group to escape?

Chapter Twelve

RIDGE

I stare at my phone screen, furrowing my brow. Why in the hell did Paige drop a pin along four eighty-eight and an Idaho license plate? I try to call and text her, with no answer.

Hopping in my truck, I drive in her direction, wondering if this is a flirtatious game or something else. My throat tightens, and the hairs on the back of my neck stand up. Fortunately, I drive armed, just in case. My cell beeps, and I see Johnny has responded to the same message because Paige shared it in our group text.

On my way

Pulling up onto the embankment behind Paige's diminutive, sleek Spider, I find Johnny standing there with his hands on his hips. His face looks dark, his expression clouded. My presence only tightens his visage as thick tension settles between us.

"What the fuck's going on?"

The cameraman shakes his head. "I got a text and assumed

110

I was being called to record more video." He scratches his head, cocking his head to the side. "I can't imagine her leaving her car like this. It looks bad."

I already know this, but my stomach still drops.

Johnny asks, "Did you notice the wet trail on the pavement?"

I shake head, reminding him, "I came from the opposite direction that you."

He shrugs. "Coolant leak is my guess. But where is she? And what was up with the plate number?"

"Pop the hood," I order.

He races to the open driver's seat door, sitting down and grabbing something from the console. He holds it up for me to see. Her key fob.

"What in the fuck?"

Johnny pops the hood, and I scan the engine quickly, finding the problem. "There's a hole in her radiator. Looks like it was made with a screwdriver or something." My words feel distant, my voice far away as time slows and dread fills me.

I pull out my phone, dial her number again, and scan the woods. An almost inaudible vibrating sound fills the air. Johnny scrambles around in the vehicle, pulling something from under her seat. Paige's cell phone.

"This is a crime scene." Sickening realization crashes into me at the exact same moment my tongue pronounces the obvious.

Johnny looks at me, his face flooding with alarm. The motherfucker would be one of my primary suspects if he wasn't sitting in Paige's car, his face echoing the confusion and panic raging inside of me.

"Can you think of anything that's been going on in her life? Anything that might point us to what happened?"

He shakes his head, grimacing. "She mentioned this weird road rage incident that happened yesterday about twenty miles outside of Hollister. Said some guy in a white truck ran her up onto the embankment...."

My face twists. "Really?" *Why in the hell didn't she tell me about this?*

He nods. "And she's been investigating this really weird cult over the past few years. Phil, our executive producer, would know more about it than me."

"What kind of cult?"

"Phil's really the guy to speak to about that." Johnny shrugs. "You may not have figured it out yet, but Paige tends to avoid me. This assignment we're on together is well out of the ordinary."

Normally, I'd tell him *good fucking thing*. After all, I don't like the way he looks at her. But I've got far bigger things on my mind, and as far as I can tell, Johnny's just as harmless as Paige claimed.

"Get the sheriff's department on the phone. Let them know it's an emergency and that I want Christian on the scene with backup. While you do that, I've got a few contacts to reach out to as well."

Striding towards the edge of the woods, I click into my favorites, where I have my Army Ranger brother, Wolfe, on speed dial. He answers on the second ring, a newborn wailing softly in the background. "Ridge."

"Sorry for the bad timing, bro. But I have an emergency."

"Let me go in the other room." I hear rustling and foot-steps on speaker as I text him the pin and message Paige dropped.

"What's this?" he asks.

"The current location of Paige's car. You know, the hot, black-haired beauty I met last night at Stonie's."

"Okay... And an Idaho license plate?"

"Roger that."

I hear fast-paced clicks coming from his keyboard.

112

"Her key fob was in the car, her cell phone under the driver's side seat. I pace around, realizing I need a second look at the scene, turning speaker off and pressing the phone to my ear as I scan the car. "I see possible signs of tire tracks behind her car. But not much else. She dropped the pin I sent you before going incommunicado. It looks like a possible abduction or..." I can't say the rest, my voice thickening and growing raw.

Over my left shoulder, I hear Johnny talking to the sheriff's department and relaying what he remembers in broken snippets. "Umm... the House of the... Shit, some number, and prophets." He pauses. "Yes, that's it. The House of the Seven Prophets. She has that reality TV show about them..."

The name hammers in my head. I have two sisters-in-law who grew up in that organization, Birdie and Faith. Both faced a horror story of intimidation, shunning, and even kidnapping before leaving the church. And Birdie had to physically escape to avoid a marriage arranged by her mother and grandmother to a much older church elder. "Do you know if the House of the Seven Prophets has any potential ties to human trafficking? Or if there was a recent reality TV show about them?"

"How do you not know about the show?" Wolfe asks.

Silence.

"Wait, one fucking minute. I thought she looked familiar at Stonie's. She's the one who interviewed all those nut jobs and cracked that organization wide open."

I answer, "Paige? Yes."

I'm not much of a TV watcher. I stay too busy for that. Wolfe knows this, so he doesn't linger long over my lack of knowledge. I exhale, "Well, they're our best lead so far..."

"I've got plenty of intel on that group. Honestly, we've been biding our time. Waiting for the perfect moment to make a move since a case involving an old Army Ranger buddy broke in Northern Idaho back in April, which makes the plate you texted me especially interesting."

"Anybody I know?"

"Who?"

"Your Army Ranger buddy?"

"Don't think so. His name is Roscoe Vaughn."

"Never heard of him."

Wolfe grunts. "The group appears to have ties with the trafficking operation we busted through Three Nations Reservation, too. So, watch your ass because those guys were no joke, and they were aligned with cartels south of the border as well as senators in D.C."

I feel sick thinking about Paige at the mercy of those kinds of men. "I can't let anything happen to her, Wolfe. She's my everything."

He pauses for a long moment. "Apparently, a lot happened after we bailed on you at Stonie's."

"You could say that."

"Alright, keep your phone handy. I'll be in touch."

"I'll have my sat phone and walkie, too."

"Five twelve," he answers my question about channels before I can even ask it. "I'll put a call into Hawk and Farzad, so we've got a pilot on standby, just in case." Both are helicopter pilots who work with Wolfe and his crew of former rangers-turned-clandestine stateside operators. Even though he's my brother, I know very little about what his supposed security company does, but our conversation is opening up my mind in vast ways. "I'll be in touch. What are you going to do in the meantime, Ridge?"

"Coordinate with the sheriff's department and possibly search and rescue before heading out to track my quarry."

There's a long pause before Wolfe says, "I've got some coordinates I'll drop your way."

"What are we talking? Headquarters? A hideout?"

"A compound deep in the woods. A site of extreme interest."

I grunt, my mind racing forward to make preparations for a manhunt.

"Stay safe, bro, and don't do anything stupid."

"Don't worry about me. Worry about the other mother-fuckers." I was made for this shit, and Wolfe knows it. But I'm also in a race against time, which lodges an acute ache in my chest.

"Roger that."

My brother, Sheriff Christian, is on his way, but I don't have time to waste. So, I tell Johnny to have Christian call me when he arrives. I jump in my truck and speed away, getting Phil Conners on the phone. Fortunately, he gave me his number earlier during negotiations. He answers on the third ring, and I dive into relaying the most essential information before interrogating him.

He tells me about the reality TV show Paige worked on and how it crossed paths with the cult. He describes her many police reports and the inept work of law enforcement to prose-cute those involved. I haven't had many personal dealings with the House of the Seven Prophets, but according to my sisters-in-law, Birdie and Faith, the church has ties in elite places throughout the nation. They also have a large presence in Hollister.

Dread seeps into my bones as I wonder why Paige never mentioned this to me. But then again, she didn't even give me her real name until she was forced to do so. If I had known more, I would have never let the woman out of my sight. Maybe that's part of the reason she was reluctant to confide in me.

As I wrap up with Phil, Sheriff Christian's call comes through, and I switch lines, filling him in. He's got search and rescue under the leadership of Logan dispatched and working the woods with their canines. I forward him Wolfe's coordinates, too. I don't know if that kind of interagency sharing is kosher, but I don't fucking care at this point. I need to find my woman before it's too late.

At my place, I load up on firearms and camouflage before racing outside to hook the trailer with my ATV to the truck. Apart from the first leg of the trip, Wolfe's coordinates cover plenty of impassable ground, at least by truck, rendering the ATV necessary. My plan balances on the knife's point of speed and stealth to get me as close to Paige's final destination as possible.

I'm running on faith and optimism, knowing I may be headed on a wild goose chase. I can't vouch for the intel, feeling like I'm pulling on random threads to find the loose one. But I can't sit on the sidelines and wait for information from others, either.

No man on this search is as invested as I am. I will find Paige if it's the last fucking thing I do. The only solace I feel as I head out to hunt is knowing the expiration date on the motherfuckers who threatened and kidnapped Paige is fast approaching. If I have my way, they'll wish they were never born.

Normally, acquiring a target requires careful planning and reconnaissance. In the Corps, I pored over maps, photographs, and other intelligence, identifying observation posts and potential target locations. I prefer being involved in this process, but I'm out of time. Nevertheless, Wolfe and his crew know their shit, and as far as I've been able to surmise, they're still neck deep in black ops. So, I couldn't ask for a better group of men to work with.

What I do have control over? Stealth and camouflage. Years of working as an outfitter leading hunts have only honed these skills. After all, most humans are clueless when it comes to elements of pursuit, like the smell of a predator downwind or the feel of someone or something's energy as it stalks you. But animals use all of their senses equally. Having learned how to circumvent their finely honed pursuit detection gives me a distinct edge.

I drop the truck off in a concealed location near four eighty-eight before unloading the ATV and disappearing into the thick forest. As I draw closer to Wolfe's coordinates, I make mental notes of potential escape routes and fallback positions. That said, I won't take advantage of any of these without Paige's security ensured.

Normally, I'd have a spotter with me who communicates shot coordinates and any other intel I might need. But there's no time for this. That said, if and when I converge with Wolfe's group, I'll likely work with Rutger, an Army Ranger sniper with a confirmed kill list that could go toe-to-toe with mine any day.

The brush thickens as I draw closer to my target location, and I find a good spot to ditch the ATV before heading in on foot. A paved road about ten miles downhill would take me straight to the compound, but my approach is all about stealth and concealment.

In the deep woods with my gear and green, black, and brown face paint, I can easily disappear as well as get much closer than these motherfuckers could ever fathom. They have no idea who they're messing with.

Maintaining a safe distance, I hunker down, and the waiting game begins. I observe activities and track movements on the property using my Leupold Mark 4 tactical rifle scope, identifying key participants and reporting back to Wolfe.

"Never seen a stranger mix of pious-looking, bearded motherfuckers and tatted cartel members."

Wolfe growls. "Yep, we've had eyes on the facility for the past few months, partially because of your girlfriend's series."

"Guess it's time to watch TV."

"Have you seen the short, fat dude that looks like a cherub?"

I grunt my reply.

"That's your main target."

"Seriously? He's a fucking Cabbage Patch."

"More like Chucky. Christian pulled some strings to gain access to Paige's cell phone and found a series of harassing texts from a number associated with this little marshmallow. And as her investigative work on the series showed, he may look harmless, but don't underestimate the fucker."

"So, he's a target I can engage?"

"We need him alive for questioning."

I growl, working hard to maintain control. "In that case, the fucker is gonna wish he'd never been born."

"Stand down, Ridge. Do not engage until we're on-site, and don't do anything that impacts our ability to question him. After that, he's all yours."

I sigh with relief. Sometimes, justice can only be served outside of conventional means. I'm glad Wolfe gets this.

"Maintain your position, and don't do anything rash. We'll be there shortly."

"What the fuck is taking so long?"

"Coordinating the bird and breach explosives." The thought of explosives anywhere near Paige makes me feel nauseous. But the compound is designed for tactical defense, which narrows our options.

"Looks like they have something going on with trucks coming in and out. What the hell do you think they're loading?"

"Drugs or humans."

"For church-going motherfuckers, they're pretty damn nefarious," I observe coolly. Surveying a line of trucks, I see activity around a white dually. Two suited men open the passenger-side door to the extended cab, pulling a woman from their vehicle. The sight of her navy trousers, brown loafers, and navy and white striped shirt makes my heart stop. Her hands are cuffed behind her, and there's a sack over her head.

My trigger finger itches to make the men leading her inside pay. But even if I take out both targets of opportunity, there's no way I could reach her from my current position, securing her in time. Instead, I watch as they escort her inside, roughly pulling her along by the arms. I see red, fantasizing about skinning each man alive. They deserve that and worse. Anybody dealing in human flesh does, but especially anyone touching my woman. I use the scope to peer into the compound's windows, gaining a sense of where she's being taken.

"I have eyes on Paige. Two suited men led her into the northwest side of the compound."

"Makes sense," Wolfe grunts. "We've surmised they have interrogation rooms and holding cells on that side. Paige's interviews for the show further confirm this."

"I need to get her the fuck out of here, Wolfe. If anything happens to her, I won't be able to live with myself."

"Stand the fuck down, bro." His voice has a hard edge to it.

"But if this were Izzie—"

"If this were Izzie, I'd do things right. I guarantee you, bro, we *will* do this right. But there are a lot more lives at stake than Paige's. Timing and strategy are everything. Besides, nobody knows how to handle these goons better than your girl."

Wolfe's words mean to comfort me, but I'm beside myself with worry. It takes every ounce of control not to storm the building myself, but that would be a suicide mission. I need to get my head on straight, calm the fuck down. But the effort feels impossible.

Never have I fought for something more precious. There's nothing I wouldn't do or sacrifice to ensure Paige's safety. As nighttime settles and the black of night covers me, I stalk closer and closer until I'm well-positioned to engage any targets that exit the compound.

I breathe a sigh of relief as Wolfe confirms his men are in position. Glancing up at the North Star, last night feels like a million years ago. I send another silent prayer heavenward that Wolfe's plan will go off without complication.

The sound of brush next to me catches my attention, and I grip my combat knife, ready to noiselessly engage, but Wolfe has already warned me to look for Rutger.

To my left, he appears, soundless and fully camouflaged. Our range is too close for words, but I nod in his direction, thankful shit's finally getting real.

Chapter Thirteen

PAIGE

I came to Rough & Ready Country to negotiate the details of a reality TV program with Ridge Dawson. Instead, I find myself at Mortimer Cady's beck and call, discussing the minutiae of *Growing Up Penitent*, the award-winning unscripted documentary series that Phil halted production on after I stumbled into a hornet's nest of illegal activities.

The odd little man with a rotund face and frame, an appearance that hides the monster beneath, dives into script choices and editing with me. I defend cuts and quotes, camera angles, and characterizations, barely able to grasp the surreal situation.

As we pour over three seasons, I become increasingly aware the man is both psychotic in his perception of others and grandiose in his self-appraisals. He becomes increasingly forceful and unhinged, and my stomach twists and knots, as his dark side emerges.

The threats he's sent me via text since leaving Los Angeles are anything but toothless. And the glares of the bearded men who serve him, wearing their telltale black and white suits, fill me with foreboding.

My only hope is that Ridge or law enforcement have found my car and phone. There should be enough evidence available to start a missing persons investigation. Still, it feels like time is running out. The sense of dread increases as evening falls. The compound's lights come on, illuminating the otherwise dark woods that press us in on all sides.

I sit in a small interrogation room with no decor and only the most modest furnishings, two chairs on either side of a table. It reminds me of the rooms where prisoners consult their attorneys in TV shows, except it has a narrow window at the top opening out onto the well-lit grounds of the compound.

My eyes strain towards it each time Cady and his entourage leave the room, turning out the lights in my room. The window glares from the exterior illumination, but I long for the pristine dark skies and stars of last night. Closing my eyes, I remember the feel of Ridge's arms around me.

I remember how he told me to find Polaris, the North Star. His words echo through my mind: *so you'll always know where to go.* If I could only see a star or two now, it would comfort me despite my present circumstances.

I've had at least three visits from Cady. When the lights come back on this time, I startle, lifting my head from the table where I fell asleep. The handcuffs have been removed from my hands, which sit folded in my lap.

"Ms. Laurier, I had rather hoped we would have come to an agreement at this point that we both feel is workable. But I'm quite frankly frustrated with your answers. To put it mildly, you're running out of time." Whack! He backhands me across the cheek without warning, snagging my lip on one of my lower canines and making it bleed.

"I don't know what you want from me," I sob, tentatively

licking my bottom lip and looking down. I taste salty, metallic blood and feel the sting of broken skin.

"I want a reboot of the show with the church cast in the proper light and my reputation restored. Or better yet, I want the show retracted altogether and a full apology from you stating that the supposed 'reality TV' you purported to show in the series was anything but that. I would like the public to go back to being unaware, thinking the House of the Seven Prophets doesn't exist at all."

Ironic. Cady wants to take the same tack as the devil—wielding non-existence as the ultimate alibi. I can't recall which author first said that. C.S. Lewis, maybe? But I remember the notion distinctly from one of my college lit classes.

I repeat, exhausted by my own words. "I am only an assistant producer at In the Haystack. But I'm more than certain Phil Conners, my boss, can address your concerns."

"I'm not hearing impaired, Ms. Laurier. You've made this claim several times today. But I know you have more power than that."

"Alright, then. You've got me. I'll amend the scripts, reshoot the series, and issue an apology. Whatever you need."

Cady shakes his head, sitting back in his chair across from me and crossing his arms. Despite his cold, aloof demeanor, there's something ridiculously impotent about his face. He could be an ugly cupid, for God's sake. But the strange incongruence between his outward appearance and inner character somehow makes him even more dangerous and unpredictable.

"I get the impression you're saying this just to make me happy and perhaps secure your freedom."

I fight the urge to bury my head in my hands and sob. The man has worn me down through exhaustion and repetition. It feels like brainwashing, reminding me of some of the witness accounts I captured while working on the TV show.

He sees weakness in me, and he's exploiting it. I have to dig deep, find grit and determination and take a different tack with him.

I take a deep, fortifying breath. "Look, Elder Cady, negotiations are all about getting what we both want, and I can tell you right now, a series reboot won't sell without requisite drama. You have to understand this as well as I do, considering your recent brush with celebrity."

He puffs out his chest ever so slightly, and I fight the disdain that tries to capture my face. The only fame he's ever known is infamy, getting castigated on my series.

Boom! A deep, percussive sound shakes the walls of the room. Instinctively, I dive to the ground. Boom! Boom! Boom! I press my palms to my ears, feeling the floor shake, too. The room fills with thick dust and smoke, and I scan it frantically.

Cady's entourage reel from the kinetic waves of the explosions before scrambling to their feet and piling around him. They scream out orders, hellbent on spiriting the man to the tunnels. *What in the hell do they mean by tunnels?* Overhead, I hear the whir of helicopter blades and then the high-pitched hum of live rounds.

Frantic male voices break out, "He's hit! Elder Cady's been hit!"

All I can do is cling to the smooth surface of the floor, breathing shallowly to avoid coughing in the fine silt from debris that dances in the air.

"Target secured!" An authoritative male voice booms.

Another orders, "Face down on the ground. Hands behind your heads." The compound falls eerily quiet, apart from the feathery sounds of whimpers and gasps and the angry thud of combat boots on cement.

My heart wobbles precariously, thrumming and floating around in my chest. Palms pressed to my ears, I register hot tears streaking down my cheeks as I pray for rescue, uncertain of what's going on.

More male voices fill the compound screaming, the sounds of aggressive footfalls shattering the air. "Face down! Hands behind your heads!"

Action swirls around me as my numb brain slowly processes what the masculine voices order. I tentatively slide my hands from my ears to the back of my head, my body trembling as I wait, breathing hard. My face kisses the cold concrete floor.

"Paige!" I hear Ridge's voice as clear as day, and my stomach knots with dread. Is this a dream? Have I already died? All I know is the sound of my mountain man's voice is far too good to be true. This can't be possible.

"Paige!" This time, the single-syllable word is accompanied by strong hands that pull me from the ground. A burly man concealed in camouflage from head to toe, with his face painted green, brown, and black, pulls me possessively into his cross-legged lap, and I wrap my arms around him, squeezing him frantically like a buoy in a tsunami. My hands and arms feel simultaneously desperate to hold him and too weak to do it effectively.

"Ridge," I pant between sobs.

"Yes, Ducky, it's me. Are you hurt?"

I stop moving for a moment, focusing hard to reassemble my scattered mind into one thinking whole. "I don't know," I whisper, my voice trembling so hard that my words sound unintelligible. "My ears are ringing. But I think that's it."

"I'm sorry," he whispers, pulling me covetously against his hard chest. "I should have never let you out of my sight. And I'm sorry for the explosives, but it was the only way into this compound. There are tunnels underneath the facility filled with women and children. The other guys are going to need help securing survivors. But first, I have to know you're okay."

I nod, leaning back slightly to stare into his face in the flickering, failing lights of the interrogation room. "No one hurt me, Romeo, I promise."

His eyes rest on my bruised cheek and bloody lip, his fingertips coming up tentatively to brush it with his thumb. Furious anger sears his gaze, his jaw tightening until I can hear the enamel of his teeth grinding together.

"Cady did that," I correct. "But that's all. He was interrogating me when the loud noises started." I shudder at the memory. "He said I was running out of time, and he seemed so angry. You saved me, Ridge."

"I targeted the motherfucker myself, although he's still alive for questioning. I will never let another man hurt you. Ever. I swear it on my life."

"Thank you," I gasp, sinking against him. "Thank you for saving me."

His lips cover mine gently, mindful of my split lip. But I don't care. I'm out of my mind with need as I crash into his mouth in return, feeling the paint on his face smudge onto my cheeks and lips.

"I was so scared," I confess, my voice trembling. "My life kept flashing before my eyes, and suddenly, I saw all my regrets as clear as day." I palm his cheeks, looking at the Marine in his deadly painted face. I fight back a sob. "I barely know you, Ridge, and this may seem completely insane. But my number one regret was not telling you how much you mean to me. I love you, Ridge Ansel Dawson."

His brows furrow, his eyes red with emotion. "And I love you, Paige Annalise Laurier, forever."

My arms snake around his neck, pulling him as close as possible as my tongue sweeps into his mouth, claiming him as aggressively as he claimed me in the hotel room.

All the superficial worries I had about my career and what other people think, never mixing business with pleasure, and barely knowing this man evaporate in the unequivocal epiphany of his arms—the one place I'm always meant to return to.

His hands palm my body, checking me for other signs of injury, and I relish the feel of his strong, comforting flesh on mine. But my mind tugs me back to reality. After all, I'm far from the only victim of the House of the Seven Prophets. "Cady's men mentioned tunnels, and so did you."

Ridge's hands stop, and he levels his gaze on me. "Yes, those motherfuckers led us right to them in their attempt to spirit him out. Hold on one moment." Ridge contacts Wolfe, confirming he has me safely as I listen, knitting my brows.

"I want to help with retrieving the survivors," I say in a wispy voice after he ends the call.

His eyes betray shock. Shaking his head, he says, "No, you've already been through too—"

"I want to help the other survivors," I repeat firmly. "*This* is the culmination of years of work for me. I have to see with my own two eyes what this cult of horrors was up to."

His eyes narrow, his face hardening, but then he shakes his head. "I can tell there's no arguing with you. You've made up your mind already."

"I have." I lift my chin resolutely.

"Okay, but only after I get confirmation that this location is fully secured."

"Thank you. I need to help the survivors ... uncover once and for all the sick secrets of the House of the Seven Prophets."

"It goes much higher than that, Paige," he grumbles, running his hand through his thick, dark hair.

His words don't surprise me.

Once we receive confirmation that the compound is secure, Ridge and I make contact with Wolfe. I remember the big brute of a man seated at the table at Stonie's yesterday, wearing a cowboy hat.

He and Ridge dwarf me, both built like professional wrestlers. He introduces me to the man who wore the brown cowboy hat and worked the jukebox, Hawk, as well as Farzad, Rutger, Alonso, McGregor, and other men whose names seem to evaporate as soon as he says them. My mind still strains, stuck in panic mode and trembling at the stimuli around it rather than processing what's going on.

They begin the work of assessing who is in the tunnels, and I help as much as I can, overwhelmed by a gut-wrenching feeling that could curl me up into a sobbing ball if I let it. The faces of the victims display so many unfathomable human emotions, but perhaps the worst are the apathetic stares of many. They're so numb to hope that they can't acknowledge their rescue, even as it unfolds before their eyes.

As I ask victims for names, ascertaining who needs immediate medical assistance, I find many can't speak. Or if they can, they're so shell-shocked by everything that's happened that they remain silent. But their eyes and facial expressions communicate volumes. *This* is what I've been working for, and I didn't even know it.

Scanning the massive network of tunnels below ground, a cursory count quickly reaches the triple digits, and my stomach roils. The magnitude of the situation is staggering, and hours pass in a haze. Sirens fill the air as the sheriff's department, search and rescue, and ambulances arrive. I recognize the other dark-haired mountain man seated with Ridge yesterday, and he introduces himself as Logan.

As dawn creeps into the compound with its blown-out walls, Ridge wraps a protective arm around my waist, urging me to follow him. "Time to go, Ducky. There's nothing else we can do here." His voice is soft and raw, and hot tears stream down my cheeks as we walk.

"Hey," he whispers, kissing my cheek. "It's going to be okay."

I shake my head, emotion gaining a stranglehold. "No, it's not going to be okay. How could it possibly be okay with this level of human cruelty going on? Who would do this, Ridge?"

The massive mountain man shakes his head. "I've seen a lot of shit in my day. But this ... this is next-level."

"We have to do something to help them..." I don't begin to know what. Still, my mind's gears grind overtime.

"I promise we will, Ducky. But first, we need to get you cleaned up. And you need to rest. We both need to rest."

"But they pretended to be so God-fearing," I whisper as we approach a tall, handsome, blond man in a sheriff's uniform. He's clean-shaven, and his blue eyes swirl with empathy.

"It was the perfect cover," Ridge declares, stopping in front of the uniformed man. "Paige, this is my older brother, Christian McLeod. Christian, this is Paige Laurier."

He nods curtly. "Nice to meet you, Ms. Laurier. Ridge tells me your actions today have been heroic and selfless despite the difficult circumstances."

"I want to do more," I say breathily, my mind festering with images of those who were trafficked. Every age. Every race. Every state of health and even those who didn't make it.

"There'll be plenty of time for that later. This problem isn't going away anytime soon. Can I give you two a lift to your truck?"

Ridge nods. "Thank you, brother," he says, stepping forward to grip him in a bear hug. "My ATV's about two miles that way in the brush. I'll be back for it later."

The blond nods. "Let's get you guys out of here."

"Hey," a gruff voice captures our attention. Turning, I see Wolfe approaching. He hugs Ridge tightly before saving a more reserved and gentle embrace for me. "Good work, Devil Dog."

"Same to you, Ranger."

The giant of a man says to me, "Sorry our first official meeting had to be under these circumstances. But I want to commend you for your bravery and tireless work on *Growing Up Penitent*. It helped us immensely in preparing for this operation, although we had originally planned for everything to go down in a couple more weeks. Some of the interviews you did, particularly with survivors, gave us the intel to make this a success. If you'd ever like to put your investigative skills to work outside of the television industry, I'd love to explore bringing you onto the team."

Ridge's face tightens. "I don't want Paige anywhere near danger again."

Wolfe frowns.

I counter. "Thank you for your concern, Romeo. But I'd like to think about this further. All I've ever wanted to do is help other people through my work. So, I'd like to revisit this offer with you after I've had some time to process everything."

"Romeo?" Christian says, the corners of his mouth turning up. He waggles his eyebrows at Ridge.

Wolfe quirks his mouth, teasing, "I don't want to think anymore about that. Later, Paige. Oh, and my wife, Izzie, and I would love to have you two lovebirds over for dinner when you're up for it."

Ridge looks at me quizzically, creasing his forehead.

"That sounds good. I can't wait to get to know you all better," I reply, looking from him to Christian and then Ridge. My mountain man's face relaxes, and he takes my hand, intertwining our fingers. Never has such a simple gesture felt more right or life altering.

Chapter Fourteen

RIDGE

Christian drops us off at my truck, and we say our goodbyes as Paige climbs into the cab, burying her head in her hands. Her soft sobs fill my ears as I get into the driver's seat, pulling her into my arms. I can feel the warm salt of her sorrow wetting my shirt.

"You're safe with me," I comfort her, stroking her silky black hair and kissing the top of her head.

"I was so scared, Ridge. I didn't know what was going to happen... And all I could think about was you and all of the things I left unsaid between us."

"I'll never let anything happen to you again. I was out of my fucking mind with worry."

She straightens, looking into my eyes. "How did you know where to find me? Did you get my pin and message?"

"Yes, but obviously, that wasn't enough to go on..."

"No. So, you called your foster brothers?" She knits her forehead.

I nod. "Wolfe's a former Army Ranger, and his buddy Rutger is, too."

"And Hawk?"

"A National Guard helicopter pilot."

"And Farzad?"

"A combat interpreter who worked with Wolfe, Rutger, Alonso, and McGregor in Afghanistan. He's also a decent helicopter pilot when Hawk's got his hands full backing up search and rescue or flying for the hospital."

"Wow," she says, shaking her head and eyeing me. "You have an army on standby. I don't know what would have happened to me if you weren't there." She pauses. "No, I know exactly what would have happened. I would have ended up like the people in the tunnels. Despite so many years of research and the things that started coming to light in my interviews, I still can't fully grasp the magnitude of this evil."

"I know," I confess. "If it were up to me, I would have shielded you from it all. I never want you to be confronted by nightmares like this. But as Wolfe said, you were instrumental in bringing this horror show to light."

"Some of those children. They couldn't have been more than toddlers. They wore diapers. All of us have been made to believe slavery ended with the Civil War, but that isn't true. Not at all." Her eyes fill with tears, and her face strains to stay composed.

"There's nothing more we can do right now, Paige."

"What's next, then?"

"Showers, food, sleep. Whatever you need to feel better."

She replies resolutely, "What I need is you, Ridge."

"You have me, Ducky. For the long haul."

"And apparently, I have that nickname, too."

I chuckle. "Yeah, as far as I'm concerned, it's a done deal."

The corners of her mouth turn down.

"At least it's not as embarrassing as Romeo. Did you see the looks on Wolfe and Christian's faces? I'll never live that shit down."

"You have a point," she giggles, turning in her seat and buckling her belt. "Take me home, mountain man."

"You don't have to ask twice," I reply, grabbing her hand and holding it atop the center console as I drive.

At my place, Paige's eyes scan over the living room and kitchen. But I can tell she's still stuck in the recent past, reliving horrific visions and things no person should ever have to see rather than observing what's right in front of her. I know what it's like to have my brain torment me this way, and staying in the present through tactile touch helps the most.

So, I lead her into my bedroom, helping her undress before we get into the shower together. She dissolves in my arms, sobbing some more as I tenderly clean her, making mental notes of the bruises on her body. It fleshes out the full picture of what she's been through. But thankfully, no one assaulted or injured her in a way that requires medical attention.

I don't know how long we spend under the hot water with me holding her, but eventually, her sobs soften. The great gasps and trembles coming from her body subside, and she looks up through a haze of tears, palming my bearded cheeks and saying, "Thank you. This is exactly what I need."

My heart warms at her words, grateful that I know how to comfort her. I realize with elated trepidation that she's my world now. As much as this epiphany thrills me, I've also never been so vulnerable to getting hurt.

"What else can I do for you? To make you feel better?"

"I need you, Ridge. I need you to make love to me."

My breath catches in my throat, and I reply in raw tones, "Done."

I turn off the water and lead her carefully out of the shower stall onto the puffy white shower mat. I use big, gray towels to dry every inch of her, including her hair. Temptation overwhelms me, and my mind races with all the ways I could take her. But I push these thoughts aside, focusing on how best to communicate tenderness and comfort to her.

Leading her to my California King, I pull back the white fluffy duvet, encouraging her to climb under the covers. Then, I head to the fireplace, kneeling naked as I start a blaze. Her eyes devour me as I work, ratcheting up my need for her to the point of pain. But caring for her will always come first.

I light candles on the nightstands on either side of the bed, fully aware that my cock's rock hard and at full attention. She eyes it thirstily, making my heart beat raucously around in my chest.

"Can I give you a massage?" I ask. "To help you relax?"

"What kind of massage?" she replies saucily, still staring at my cock.

"You'll see."

She nods, peeking at me playfully from the covers.

"I mean to do things right with you. My own needs can wait," I say firmly. "But I don't have massage oil or anything along those lines because, like I said before, I don't do one-night stands or casual hookups. And until last night, I was going through a very extended dry spell."

"Me, too," she confesses with a giggle. "Do you have any coconut oil by chance?"

"Like for cooking?"

She nods.

"I do."

"It should make a good massage oil, although you'll have to heat it with your hand so that it melts."

"I can do that," I say, my bare feet padding off towards the kitchen.

I return with a bowl brimming with the white, hard stuff, and she laughs.

"What?"

"That's probably enough for ten massages."

"Well, I figure we can use it as lube, too," I wink.

"Not that I'll need lube with the way you turn me on, Romeo."

"Oh yeah?"

"Yeah." She grins like the Cheshire Cat. "I'm already dripping."

I grip the bowl of coconut oil so tightly I fear it'll break in my hand. Taking a few deep breaths to get my pulsating cock back under control, I answer, "You don't even know what wet is yet. Lie back and let me spoil the hell out of you."

Her eyes brim with tears as she searches my face.

"What's wrong?" I whisper.

She shakes her head. "You're just so perfect for me. Like you were made for me, even though we seemed so different at first. How do you know exactly what I need?"

"Because this and this," I say, motioning from my heart toward hers. "Are connected now. In ways that can never be broken or altered. Forever, Paige."

"Forever."

"Lie on your stomach," I order gently, and she obeys without question, her cheeks happily glowing. I straddle her on the bed, hovering over her, my cock playfully teasing her ass cheeks and lower back as I warm a gob of coconut oil in my hand before drizzling it over her back.

She shudders and inhales at the sensation. Then, I cover her with my large, rough hands, palming her firmly to let her know where I am before I start massaging her with my fingers and forearms. I work the immense tension slowly from her shoulders, neck, and back as she alternates between exclamations of pleasure and grimaces. I dig into the stress, working it out of her body slowly and methodically.

Covering every inch of her back, shoulders, neck, and arms, I follow more intense pressure with gentle kisses. Paige melts into the mattress somewhere between the tension of the deep tissue work and my feather-light caresses as I move lower, massaging her ass cheeks, the backs of her thighs, and then her calves and feet.

"How in the hell did you learn to massage like this?" she questions.

I chuckle. "Well, before I enlisted in the Corps, I worked a couple of summers up at the ski resorts around Tahoe doing massages."

She turns her head to eye me. "So, you started out rubbing on ski bunnies."

"Never like this, of course," I correct, my cheeks burning. "But yeah, I was trained in deep-tissue massage, and I worked with a mixture of men and women. It was enough to make me go into the Marines because beyond you and my family, I don't like people much."

She giggles, looking over her shoulder at me. "So, I have my own private masseuse."

I nod, adding earnestly, "You're the only person I will touch this way for the rest of my life."

"I like the sound of that."

"And I like making you feel good," I say.

"You make me feel amazing," Paige declares in seductive, dark tones. "But I'm curious about something."

"What?"

"I want to see what coconut oil does as a lube."

A growl resonates up from my chest, and my pained cock, stiffens even more, the response to her request throbbing and painful.

"Hmm... First, I need to finish massaging the front of you." I raise up on my knees. "Turn over for me, Annalise."

"Annalise," she snickers. "Yes, Ansel."

She complies, and I feel like I'm going to fucking explode all over her belly as I stare at her ample tits. But years in the Corps have taught me discipline and to deny my bodily needs.

Instead, I grab another handful of coconut oil, warming it and massaging it into the fronts of her shoulders, her upper chest, and her arms down to her individual fingers.

My hands glide over her, gauging the pressure by the look on her face, and I won't even think about indulging my needs until I've covered every inch of her with attention, finishing with a toe massage that has her lying in bed like a pile of limp spaghetti, her eyes closed, her face bliss-filled.

I lift her right foot, taking her big toe into my mouth as shivers of pleasure visibly run up and down her core.

"God, that feels so good, Ridge. You're going to make me come, and you haven't gone anywhere near my pussy."

I'm not much of a bragger, but when it comes to Paige, I need her to remember who I am. "And you didn't even know a man could make you come before you met me."

She nods deliriously, her eyes rolling back in her head as I suck her toes one by one in and out of my mouth, massaging her foot with my hands before switching sides. My cock drips pre-cum, and I focus hard on self-control as I make my way slowly up her body, spreading her legs for my feast.

But first, she needs a little more teasing. I grab another fingerful of the coconut oil, letting it warm in my palm before teasingly dribbling it over her clit and pussy. She gasps, breathing harder.

A high-pitched sigh escapes Paige's lips as my fingers spread her labia, and my head lowers. Teasingly, I let her feel my warm breath, watching with delight as her channel tightens. Damn, I have nearly taken this woman to orgasm without even touching her pussy or pearl.

"Yes, Ridge," she screams. "I need you so much. Make me yours."

I exhale again, watching her spasm and reveling in the way her body responds to me. "Your pussy already is all mine," I declare. Sinking into her, I swirl her nub with my tongue, hungry for her tangy, musky flavor. "Mine," I growl, swiping my tongue across her slit. "Mine," I repeat, doing it again as her hips strain towards my face, begging for more.

How any man ever had her convinced she couldn't come, I'll never know. But I'm happy for their ineptitude, which kept her searching for a man who won't settle for anything less than her total surrender to bliss.

I tease and slurp her clit, dragging my tongue through her dripping folds before I add a finger and then two, stroking and petting her pussy until it flutters and quivers against my fingers. Her juices grow slicker and more plentiful as I suck her clit and play with her lips, alternating swipes and swirls of my tongue.

I work her G-spot with increasing intensity, delighting in the way her channel swells around me, gripping and sucking me in as I push her over the edge. She screams my name, digging her fingernails into the mattress. I make a promise to myself that next time, those fingers will be clawing my back.

Paige lies in a delectable pile of satisfaction as I inch up her oily body, kissing and licking my way to her mouth. I claim her frantically, finally letting my own needs take over as she tastes herself on my lips and beard. Her arms thread around my neck, pressing me passionately against her as my arms hook under her thighs, sliding her legs up to make my entrance easy.

I slip into her slowly, savoring the way her drenched, aroused pussy takes and holds me. "Fuck," I whisper, letting my hips lead as I move in and out of her, from tip to balls, memorizing every inch of her honeyed perfection. I could happily die in her fucking pussy. It's a bizarre thought to have. But it's the goddamn truth.

Her fingers trace their way down my neck to my upper back, the intensity of her grip increasing as I deepen my thrusts, seizing her hips and angling them to target her pleasure center with the tip of my cock. Her head lolls back, her breath escaping in great sighs as I stroke her to perfection, feeling her shiver and tremble around me and knowing I'm about to take her there again.

My cock's past the point of pain, so fucking needy I clench my jaw, gritting my teeth to hold on. But I'm a greedy motherfucker, and I won't be satisfied until I make her come undone again. Until I make her drench my cock in her sweet juices.

"Ridge!" she screams, writhing beneath me and coming so hard it pushes me over the edge. My pelvis slams into her as thick waves of hot cum flood her pussy, and I cry, "Paige! Fuck!"

I collapse on the bed next to her, my rod still buried to the hilt as she breathes hard next to me, her eyes closed. She rolls towards me, throwing her arm over my chest. Kissing my pecs and tracing my tattoos with her petal-soft fingertips, she adores me, making me feel more loved and wanted than I ever have before.

It puts tears in my eyes, fortifying my commitment to protect and keep her for all eternity. We caress and stroke each other, reveling in the sensations of being together ... of being loved. She whispers secrets and plans to me, stuff I get the impression she hasn't told another living soul, and I return the favor, bearing my heart completely to her.

Fully relaxed and headed towards sleep, silence fills the room. Yet, I get the sudden impression Paige's mind is whirring with thoughts.

Looking down at her, I ask, "What's on your mind, Pretty Lady?"

"Would you be mad at me if I consider Wolfe's offer of working as an investigative researcher for his group?"

I groan, unable to think beyond my selfish need to keep her safe. But the topic goes with something else that's on my mind. "Only if he can ensure me you'll never be in danger."

She nods, smiling ambiguously. "I need to find ways to

continue fighting this fight. And I want to do it more effectively than reality TV production alone. That said, I won't abandon you or your show."

"The show? Honestly, it's the furthest thing from my mind right now." I clear my throat. "I've also been thinking about ways I can help out more by working with my brother's group."

"But that would put you in harm's way."

I pause, relishing in the way her hands jealously grip me. I'm not used to being needed and wanted this way. "Yes, but I have unmatched training that makes me perfect for this line of work. And there's so much that needs to be done. I had no idea until we went in the tunnels tonight."

"I know," she sighs. "What would you think about adopting some of the children if they can't be reunited with their parents?"

"Wow." I sigh sharply. I feel equal parts elated that she's planning a future and a family with me, even as I hesitate about making such a life-changing decision. "With you? Yes, Ducky. I'd consider it."

Her eyes open, blurry with tears, as she whispers, "That brings me to another thing..."

I incline my head, letting her know I'm listening.

"Military Mountain Man, I know you were hesitant to sign over rights to your show for a season. But the contract I want is much more personal and much longer."

"Oh, yeah? What do you have in my mind, Ms. Laurier?"

"A lifetime contract with a few stipulations. You know, what we like to refer to in the business as the fine print."

"Oh, shit. Here it comes. Lay it on me."

"For starters, a name change is in order and a permanent relocation."

"To where?"

"Where it all began, Rough & Ready Country."

I chuckle.

"What, are you going bashful on me again?"

I lightly brush my fingertips over her cheek, penetrating her soul with my eyes. "A part of me will always feel a little bashful around you."

She looks surprised. "And why's that?"

"Because you're the most beautiful thing I've ever seen and ever will see."

"And how can you be so sure of that?"

"I'm sure."

She giggles, stroking my beard. "You haven't even asked about the name change. I thought that would be one of the bigger points to negotiate."

"Well, you have to tell me about it first," I tease.

"Laurier to Dawson," she says in a whisper.

"Laurier to Dawson," I repeat, looking up at the ceiling. "It sounds like you're proposing to me."

"Could be."

"Where's my ring?"

She laughs.

Leaning in, I capture her mouth for a long, soulful kiss. "How about you leave the proposing and the ring to me?"

She smiles brilliantly, her cheeks coloring. "Well, I am a master negotiator, so I figure I'll get a head start on our contract."

"Oh, there will be no negotiating on this subject," I inform her gruffly.

She arches her eyebrow. "And why not?"

"Because I want you ... all of you for the rest of my life, and I won't settle for anything less." Emotion colors my voice.

"Good," she whispers, tears threatening to spill over her bottom lashes. "Because you're my one non-negotiable, too."

~

Looking for more from Paige and Ridge, including the mountain man's official proposal? Read an exclusive bonus scene here: https://www.engrideaves.com/freebies/

Intrigued to learn more about Aspen and Axel's story in *Love at First Secret*? Get the full scoop on this steamy read here: https://www.engrideaves.com/love-at-first-secret

Did you enjoy this spicy, fast-paced mountain man romance? If so, check out the Rough & Ready Country series, jam-packed with steamy cowboy mountain man and curvy girl love. Explore the series free in KU: https://amzn.to/43zZCzO

Join the Engrid Eaves Community!

RUGGED, POSSESSIVE COWBOY MOUNTAIN MEN.
HEADSTRONG, COURAGEOUS, CURVY GIRLS.
STEAMY, SATISFYING HAPPILY EVER AFTERS.
GIVEAWAYS. FREEBIES.
NEW RELEASES. LATEST NEWS.

Subscribe to my newsletter today to never miss out on a new
steamy, small-town read.
SIGN UP FOR MY NEWSLETTER

Also by Engrid Eaves

ROUGH & READY COUNTRY

Love at First Blizzard - He's a reclusive mountain man who runs a husky rescue, but his world gets turned upside down by the curvy classical musician he saves from a freak March blizzard.

Love at First Campfire - She's a headstrong, curvy true crime reporter who's never needed anybody until a handsome search and rescue unit lead risks everything to save her.

Love at First Rescue - He's a small-town sheriff who plays by the rules until his sexy dispatcher changes up the game, initiating a rescue that sets long-time passions ablaze.

Love at Second Chance - She's the new home health nurse in Rough & Ready Country, but miles of history with the grumpy ranch foreman are in danger of reigniting, despite her best intentions.

Love at First Baby - He's a wildland firefighter who refuses to settle down for anyone until the curvy hometown sweetheart and an unexpected baby make him reconsider what and who he's living for.

Love and Forgiveness - She's a museum director trying to move on until her estranged husband's security company wins her facility's contract, resurrecting long-buried passions.

Love at First Relationship - Everything about Flynn's paralegal, Jasmine, is off-limits as his much younger, inexperienced employee. But a fake relationship proposal quickly blossoms into much more.

Love at First House - A marriage of convenience is the only way to help Turner's neighbor keep her family together. He tells himself it's a practical arrangement, but his heart has other plans.

Love at First Night - He's a helicopter pilot crushing on his best friend's little sister, Roxy. A cataclysmic night gives them a glimmer into a world of possibilities, but will love or heartbreak prevail?

Love at First Beat - Army cardiologist, Fletcher, excels at healing... But matters of the heart are another thing. Until he meets Drew, a romance writer, who specializes in happy endings.

Love at First Doubt - Kindergarten teacher, Effie, knows the town bad boy, Rock, is trouble. A tattoo artist and rockabilly musician, the cowboy's all wrong for the wholesome curvy girl. Or is he?

Love at First Wild - Ridge is a wild outdoorsman mountain man who goes viral with survival videos. Paige is a TV show producer determined to make him famous. But first, she has to tame him...

Love at First Secret - When Aspen and Axel meet on the Mountain Mates dating site, sparks flame and walls go up. Both hide secrets and lack trust, threatening to crush their blossoming feelings...

Love at First Revenge

Love and Redemption

ROUGH & READY LAWMEN

Possessed by the Bounty Hunter - A six-figure bounty draws me back to my ex-fiancée and her mafia-linked Creole family. Soon, a centuries-old curse blurs the line between hunter and hunted.

LOG CABIN CHRISTMAS

Gifted to the Mountain Man - Farzad's first Christmas stateside is lonely until the woman he can't stop thinking about needs protection. As sparks fly, will his cabin and heart be big enough for two?

NAUGHTY & SPICE

Mountain Man Santa - A blizzard leaves Jerry snowed in with his curvy server, Stacey. She may not be ready for commitment...or the secrets of his dark past. But naughty or nice, he won't stop until she's all his...

About the Author

ALPHA HEROES. CURVY GIRLS.
STEAMY ADVENTURES. HEA.

Bestselling author Engrid Eaves writes steamy, fast-paced romances featuring gruff alpha male protectors and the head-strong, curvy girls they fall head over heels for.

Her heroes may have painful pasts, but they always find forever with their soulmates. Sexy, satisfying, heartfelt happily ever afters guaranteed!

If you'd like to stay in touch or get your next delicious cowboy mountain man, curvy girl romance fix (and who doesn't?), sign up for her newsletter: www.engrideaves.com.

g goodreads.com/engrideaves
BB bookbub.com/profile/engrid-eaves
instagram.com/engrid_eaves
tiktok.com/@authorengrideaves
f facebook.com/EngridEavesAuthor